THE FORGIVING HEART

Sheila Spencer-Smith

CHIVERS

British Library Cataloguing in Publication Data available

This Large Print edition published by AudioGO Ltd,
Bath, 2012.
Published by arrangement with the author.

U.K. Hardcover   ISBN   978 1 4458 4471 8
U.K. Softcover   ISBN   978 1 4458 4472 5

Printed and bound in Great Britain by
MPG Books Group Limited

AN ESCAPE FOR NICOLE

Nicole gazed down in horror as her mobile phone sank through the clear water to vanish in a mound of bladderwort on the sea bed.

It would have been safely back in her bag now, she thought, if she had boarded the Kenvarloe bus as she had intended. Instead, on impulse, she had broken her journey in this attractive Cornish town, revelling in the busy harbour, the fishing boats, sun speckled sea and golden sand.

Until her phone rang.

'Dropped something?' asked an interested voice behind her.

Startled, Nicole spun round. Bradley? Even though the man regarding her with interest was plainly a long-distance walker clad in shorts, tattered T-shirt and hiking boots he was so much like the man she wanted to avoid it was startling.

She felt warmth flood her cheeks. 'My mobile,' she said, her voice unsteady. 'It's down there. Someone phoned me . . .' Someone she never wanted to see or hear from again, someone who was convinced she didn't mean it.

He dumped his rucksack on the ground. 'No problem,' he said. 'Wait here.'

He wrenched off his walking boots,

1

pulled his T-shirt over his head and slipped effortlessly over the quayside. Seconds later he emerged, shaking a spray of water from his head before swimming with confident strokes to the steps in the harbour wall.

'Yours?' he said as she joined him.

She took it from him with trembling hands. Surely there weren't other mobiles down there, dropped by inept females? Maybe he thought she had stolen it and was on her way to get a valuation. But it couldn't be worth much. Probably the proceeds wouldn't even pay her bus fair to Kenvarloe and that was only six miles away by road.

'Salt water's lethal,' he said. 'You'll need to open it up and douse it in fresh water before it has time to corrode.'

The breath hurt her throat as she thought of the masses of green verdigris already on the attack. 'I need to save the messages,' she said. 'They're important.'

'Then get it to a phone shop quickly if there's one anywhere near.'

He looked at her in such a familiar way she shivered, reminded vividly of one of the reasons she had come to Cornwall. But Bradley didn't know she was here. That was the beauty of mobile phones and being able to leave messages on them. He had no reason to believe she had left London.

If she hadn't been so shocked at the resemblance between the two of them with

2

their broad shoulders and fair hair she could have thanked him as he deserved to be thanked.

'I'm grateful to you,' she said, struggling for control. 'It was good of you. And now you're soaked.'

'Not to worry. Spare shorts in my bag. You'll need to act quickly if your messages are crucial. Good luck.'

She stared after him as he retrieved his belongings. Surely he wasn't going to change here on the busy quayside? But no, it seemed he couldn't get away fast enough.

He must think her crazy for dropping her phone over the harbour wall and then going on about those messages. But they were the only proof she could produce of Bradley's over-friendly interest in her, if proof were ever needed.

No-one apart from herself knew about them. Certainly not her sister back there in London, worried she might lose the baby she was expecting. This was a bad time to unload her own problems on her, so instead she had pretended that she hadn't a care in the world.

The strain had been enormous.

*   *   *

Nicole located the Phone & Camera Shop in a back street leading steeply uphill from the harbour. Relieved, she pushed open the door

3

and went in.

The assistant took her mobile from her gingerly, his lips twitching. 'Taken it for a swim?' he said, eyeing her with interest through his gleaming rimless glasses.

She felt herself flush. 'Something like that.'

He opened the back. 'Can you leave it with me for three or four days and I'll see what I can do?'

Slightly encouraged, she smiled. 'Can you save the messages on it?'

'I'll do my best, m'dear. I've had plenty of practice already this season.'

'Shall I come back for it at the weekend then?

'If you can last that long without it.'

'Oh yes,' she said with feeling. 'I've no problem with that.' In fact she'd have no problem if he'd suggested four weeks instead of four days, she thought as she went back to the Kenvarloe bus stop.

*   *   *

The narrow road wound first inland and then, higher up, giving views of the sea across small stone-walled fields shining green in the late afternoon sunshine. The great sweep of land dropped away to the right and a flutter of excitement caught in Nicole's throat as they swung round yet another bend. They approached the grey cottages of Kenvarloe

4

and there was the pub and the church tower seeming to say that they had been here for centuries and didn't want to be disturbed now, thank you very much.

Nicole alighted with her bulky bags and stood for a moment breathing in the earthy smell of muddy lanes. High above her a skylark's song trilled. She looked around her for a moment, taking in the peaceful scene. No-one was about, only a languid dog that got up from his place in the sun by the churchyard wall, shook himself, gave an interested look in her direction and then sank down into slumber again.

Zelda had described the place over the phone when she first moved in so Nicole knew she had to turn her back on the village and head for the coast path until she saw a couple of cottages down on the left. She set off along an obvious track that sloped gently downhill from the church.

Walking between stone-walled Cornish hedges coated with grass and wild flowers was pleasant even with heavy bags. The scent of wild thyme mingled with honeysuckle, and beside the track a stream gurgled.

She could understand Zelda coming to live here even if her sister couldn't. But then Harriet was always the sensible one and it was hardly sensible to live a longish way from a Cornish village to open a tea shop, was it? Well no, not if you were Harriet. But if you

were Zelda it seemed a good location with the coast path not far away.

At first she had done well, but lately things hadn't been so good. Now with the latest setback it looked as if Zelda might have to sell up and move away from the area to where she could find enough lucrative work to keep her going until she retired.

Nicole raised her chin as she strode along. This wasn't going to happen if she could help it. She knew that Zelda had worked hard, her optimism carrying her through many difficulties with resource and good humour. It simply wasn't fair that hooligans trashing the place would mean the end of Zelda's dream.

She rounded a corner and looked down over land that stretched to the rugged coast and turquoise sea. And there was Zelda's home as she had described it, stone-built and so well settled into the wild hillside surrounding it that you would hardly notice it from this direction. In fact, if she stopped to take a photograph of the cottage it probably wouldn't show up at all.

Smiling, Nicole trudged on, imagining Zelda's delight that she had come to help her turn the place into the success it had once been. A spark would be ignited, she was sure of it, and then watch out, Kenvarloe, you won't know what's hit you!

She left the track to head down another towards the cottages, she could see in the distance and noticed that the door of the far

one that she knew was Zelda's, was tightly shut. No wonder, really, after the break- in, but there was a deserted feel about the place that didn't seem right.

Kenvarloe Tea Rooms, there could be no mistake.

Nicole pulled the bell rope at the side of the door but heard no sound. The door was locked and the curtains drawn across the downstairs windows to prevent anyone looking in. Since when had Zelda been so sensible? She must have been more shaken than she had let on.

She stepped back from the door and peered up at the bedroom windows. All tightly shut like the downstairs ones. Zelda was out. Or away from home? Or could it be something more sinister?

Concerned, Nicole placed her bags at the side of the porch out of sight. Then she opened the gate to the neighbouring cottage. Two sun-bleached wooden containers filled with yellow pansies stood on either side of the open door and a tabby cat sat watching her from a rickety garden seat.

At Nicole's knock a girl came running, her brown hair tied back from her face. Her long flowery skirt was topped by a short-sleeved jacket buttoned to her neck and she carried a huge shoulder bag.

'You're looking for Zelda?' she said in a surprisingly deep voice 'She won't be long if they don't get held up.'

7

'They?'

'She and Mark. They went soon after lunch.'

Nicole stared at her, bemused. 'I thought my aunt would be here.'

'They've gone to the Cash-and-Carry for a big shop. I'd ask you in but I'm just off out to meet Olaf down at Witten and I'm a bit late.'

'That's all right,' said Nicole hurriedly. 'I'll have a look round while I'm waiting now I know she won't be long. Thanks anyway.'

She went thoughtfully back to *Kenvarloe Tea Rooms*.

Tempting as it was, she had managed to bite back a startled query about Mark. She was glad she had played it cool and not let on that his existence was a surprise to her. He could be anyone . . . someone Zelda had got in to landscape the garden? Not likely in her straightened circumstances. Landscaping was the last thing she would want anyway. Or was he just an odd job man useful for accompanying her shopping this afternoon? The Cash-and-Carry could be miles away for all she knew and impossible for Zelda to get there without a lift.

The paved patio at the side of the cottage that faced the sea was edged by an escallonia hedge for extra shelter. Wooden tables and chairs were set out invitingly. Nicole sank down on one of the seats to wait for their return.

It looked as if someone had been working

recently on a raised bed nearby because it was partly planted out with small hydrangea plants. Surprising. Zelda had always poured scorn on cultivated shrubs in wild areas and the surroundings here were definitely wild. Was this Mark's doing?

Food for thought here even if hydrangeas weren't edible. Or maybe they were and she hadn't known about it. Hydrangea soup? No, too fanciful. Smiling at her foolish thoughts she looked about her.

In her recent phone calls her aunt had dwelt lightly on her dismay at finding the cottage turned upside down after the break-in and of her attempts to set it to rights.

Being Zelda she had even seen the funny side of the thugs leaving empty-handed. 'They didn't think anything of mine worth taking,' she had said in mock indignation. 'Can you imagine it, Nicole?'

Nicole could, only too well, and had worried for her aunt living alone in this remote place.

The young neighbour had told her that Zelda and Mark would be back soon but that could mean anything. The distant rocky headland would be a good place to head for in the meantime. From there she would have a clear view of a returning vehicle and would have the advantage of forming a quick opinion of this man before Zelda introduced them.

TELLING ZELDA ALL HER WOES

Nicole climbed high up on the rocks to find a suitable seat. Leaning back, she closed her eyes, enjoying the warmth of the sun on her skin and beginning to feel the tension seep out of her.

The only sounds were mewling seagulls and the mumble of a tractor in the distance. Nearer at hand bees hummed in the patches of wild thyme among the cracks in some of the lower boulders. She marvelled that they had managed to survive in such hard conditions when the plants in Zelda's flower bed looked none too happy.

After a while she opened her eyes and sat up to take in more of the glorious view of sea and sky. She could hardly believe she was here in this beautiful place free from the anxiety that had dogged her these past few weeks.

'I'll have to leave here tomorrow at seven-thirty,' she had said only yesterday in Harriet's tidy London kitchen.

Head tilted a little to one side, she had looked at her sister, waiting for her reaction and knowing what it would be.

'You're being selfish as usual, Nicole,' Harriet said. 'You know Robert will still be eating his breakfast. He never leaves for the station until eight.'

10

Nicole smiled. 'Then I'll get a taxi.'

In fact she had already booked one. Not for her Robert's last minute dash, wiping crumbs from his shirt front with one hand while driving with the other. She didn't want to listen either to any more of his advice on how to run her life.

Primed by Harriet, he would insist that what she was doing in hurrying down to Cornwall was utter madness. At twenty-four she was old enough to make her own decisions.

Harriet's lips had pursed as she picked up a biscuit crumb from the worktop and dropped it in the bin. 'So you're still insisting on going ahead with this mad scheme, Nicole?'

'If you call it mad helping out our aunt in her hour of need after all she did for us when we were young,' Nicole said.

Harriet sniffed. 'The far west of Cornwall wasn't once called West Barbary for nothing, you know. Well-named, I'd say. Barbaric then and not much better now.'

'If you say so,' said Nicole, smiling. 'Zelda doesn't know I'll be descending on her and you're not to phone and warn her. You know how she loves surprises. And promise me you won't tell anyone else either.'

'On your own head be it then.'

'I've loved staying with you, you know that, Harriet,' Nicole said with warmth. 'And instead of heading back to my own place now I'd like to help Zelda out. There's no harm in

11

that surely?'

Harriet had looked suddenly vulnerable. 'I don't like to think of you being taken advantage of, that's all.'

Nicole's voice had softened as she clasped her sister's hands. 'It'll be all right, I promise.'

Now she wriggled slightly into a more comfortable position against the rock. Hearing voices, she looked around her. The rocky outcrop that formed a landmark for miles around was on the extreme tip of the headland. From her vantage point she watched a young couple pass by with hardly a glance in her direction.

Yawning, she looked across at Zelda's cottage. There was no-one there yet or she would see a vehicle parked nearby. Her eyelids drooped. Struggling to remain alert, she got up, stretched and looked out to sea. There was a boat out there now, heading purposely this way along the coast.

'Checking its lobster pots,' called a voice from below. 'I watched it go out earlier.'

Shocked, she spun round, knowing instantly who he was.

'I didn't startle you, did I?' he said. 'Hey, are you OK?'

She shuddered and then rubbed her cheeks in an effort to appear calm and relaxed. He was so like Bradley it wasn't true. Her heart beat wildly. 'I . . . I'm all right.' She took a deep breath.

'Sit down,' he said, concern in his voice. 'I thought you'd seen me.'

She tried to laugh as she did so. 'A good thing I wasn't on the cliff edge then or you'd have had murder on your hands.'

'It's not murder if it's an accident,' he said. 'Manslaughter maybe, but only if you could prove I wanted to be rid of you. But then you wouldn't be in a position to do that, would you?'

He sounded so serious she smiled.

He retrieved his rucksack and sat down too. 'A good place this for a rest,' he said. 'The Dancing Hole.'

'What?'

'The name of this place according to the Ordnance Survey map. I understand at certain times the beams of the setting sun shine directly through it and you can imagine the rocks dancing.'

Nicole glanced round, trying to picture it. He seemed well-informed for someone just passing by. Or had he just made that up? She looked at him suspiciously and saw amusement in his eyes.

He shrugged. 'We all believe what we want to believe.'

The flat boulder at his side made a good table for the thermos flask he got out and placed there. 'Coffee?' he said, raising an enquiring eyebrow. 'Milk already in. No sugar, I'm afraid.'

13

'I don't take sugar.' She watched him pour and then took the cup from him with a murmur of thanks.

He sat with his hands round his legs staring out to sea until the coffee was cool enough to drink. Then he tipped the flask to his mouth, took a testing sip and then drank what was left. 'Daniel's the name, Daniel Murray,' he said.

'Hi, Daniel.'

He took her empty cup from her. 'I'm walking the coast path round Land's End to Lyme Regis.'

'A long way,' she agreed.

He looked searchingly at her when she didn't give her name in return. 'Not all in one day, of course.'

She nodded, unable to tell him of the sheer panic she had felt on seeing him because for a second she had believed he was someone she never wanted to see again. But this man was more suntanned than Bradley, his smile warmer. Bradley wouldn't have jumped from the harbour wall to rescue a stranger's mobile phone. Or produced a flask of coffee when he thought it was needed.

'Thanks for the drink,' she said. 'I'm fine now. It was just the shock of seeing you when I thought I was alone.'

He looked at her with a serious expression on his face, but then there was a twitch at one side of his mouth. 'Seeing me is enough to tip anyone over the edge. By the way, what did you do about your phone?'

'It was good advice you gave me,' she said. 'The phone shop said to go back in a few days. It should be fine.'

He nodded. 'They keep a special solution for accidents of that nature. I'm glad to hear that.'

He sounded as if he meant it and she was ashamed that she wanted him gone. She realised, suddenly, that she'd had nothing to eat and drink for hours. She glanced towards the cottage and then away again.

'Something wrong?' he asked, following her gaze.

'No really. I'm waiting for someone, that's all. I'll have to go.'

'And I should be on my way too.'

She stood up unsteadily, supporting herself against an overhanging rock. 'They're here now. I can see the car.'

A white vehicle was driving down the track to the cottage. Two people got out and started to unload some bags. Then the man drove away again.

'Come on then,' Daniel Murray said. 'Nothing for it but for me to escort you there to make sure you're OK since you look fit to pass out at any moment.'

She wiped her hand across her forehead. 'No, really, I can manage on my own.' To prove it she took a step away from the rock face but then, dizzy, had to cling to it again.

15

He stepped forward to help her.

'Don't touch me!'

He looked surprised at the sharpness in her voice.

'I'm sorry,' she muttered. 'It's just that . . .'

'Nothing sinister intended. I want to help, that's all.'

'I know. I'll be all right in a minute.'

She took several deep breaths and gradually the dizziness passed. With a strong effort of will she got herself down to the path and turned to look at him. 'Please go now,' she said sharply.

'With you in this state? No way.'

She shuddered, not knowing how to get rid of him. Her eyes fixed on the cottage and concentrating hard, she moved forward. She bit her lip, conscious all the time that he was close behind her.

When at last they got there he tapped smartly on the door. It swung open and Zelda Leavey in white cut-offs and sleeveless top beamed at them as if they were her favourite people in the whole world.

'Nicole!'

Immediately her left arm was round Nicole in a tight hug. 'My darling niece, this is truly wonderful.'

As her aunt released her Nicole stared, appalled, at her right arm encased in plaster. 'Zelda, what happened? What have you done?'

'Stupidly, I tripped. Luckily Olaf was around

16

to run me to hospital. They've been so kind, Olaf and Pippa. A broken wrist, would you believe?'

'You didn't tell us . . .'

'Why worry you, Nicole? You've enough to think about with Harriet's pregnancy. And I didn't expect you to come.'

'Thank goodness I did,' said Nicole in heartfelt tones.

'And now you're here and you've brought a friend.'

'No, I . . .'

She was cut short as Daniel stepped forward.

'Daniel Murray,' he said. 'I gave your niece a hand when she was feeling faint.' He looked at Nicole. 'OK now? Then I'll head off.'

'Feeling faint?' said Zelda in alarm. 'Come in, both of you. You won't get away as easily as that, young man. I need to know a bit more of what's been happening.'

He hesitated. 'I really need to get on my way to find somewhere to pitch my tent for the night.'

Zelda smiled warmly at him. 'No problem. There's grass out at the back and an outside loo. I'll have a meal ready in two ticks.'

Nicole glanced unsmilingly at him. Zelda was going way too fast. It was a wonder she didn't produce a silken web and bind him hand and foot to the door handle so he couldn't escape.

17

'I've already eaten all I need, thanks,' he said. His face lit up into a smile. 'Thank you for the offer, but I'll be off now.'

'But only as far as the back lawn?' Zelda's eyes twinkled at him.

'I'll pitch my tent on that rough piece of land beyond the wall then,' he said. 'And thanks. I'll be off at first light tomorrow.' He glanced at Nicole, seemed about to say something more but thought better of it, and left.

'Now then, Nicole dear,' Zelda said as they went inside. 'Let me look at you properly. Oh my, your face is as white as a sheet. We'll have coffee first before I see about something to eat.'

'I'll give you a hand.'

'Not a bit of it, just leave your bags where they are and go on through. I'll get you to carry in the tray when it's ready.'

To Nicole's surprise the room looked comfortable with huge piles of cushions scattered everywhere in the gaudy colours Zelda loved. A blue jug of sweet-scented honeysuckle stood in the hearth. No-one would guess that only a week ago intruders had forced an entry and roughed up the place.

She sank down on the sofa and listened to the sounds of her aunt making coffee with her uninjured hand and humming softly as she did so.

Zelda was always loving and kind. She had

focused a lot of attention on her husband's small nieces and had never lost touch even when Uncle Jem died. No blood relation could have been more devoted to her than Zelda or more concerned for her welfare. Nicole wondered now that she hadn't told her about Bradley before, but the physical distance between them had made her hesitate.

In no time at all the coffee was made. Nicole carried in the tray and put it down on a handy table. Then she pulled forward a low chair for her aunt.

'Now, dear, are you going to tell me what's bothering you?' said Zelda. 'It can't be anything to do with your young friend surely?'

'Not really apart from looking like the man who's been a bit of a nuisance lately.'

Then it came out in a rush, urged on by Zelda's concern. 'You poor, poor girl,' she said at last, her voice deep with sympathy. 'I can understand this Bradley chap finding you attractive, a pretty girl like you, but then to keep pestering you . . .'

'I don't think he could quite believe that I wasn't interested in him,' said Nicole. 'His phone calls kept coming, some of them quite nasty. He left messages . . . I kept them in case I ever needed them for proof or anything.'

Zelda looked appalled. 'But it's not going to come to that if I have anything to do with it, I promise.'

Nicole leaned forward to pour the coffee

19

and placed Zelda's cup and saucer within easy reach of her. 'As soon as the school holidays started I packed my bag and went to Harriet's. Then your break-in gave me the perfect reason for coming down here right away and no questions asked.'

'It's so nice to be useful.'

'Oh no, I didn't mean that.'

The dimple in Zelda's cheek deepened as she smiled. 'I know you didn't, dear.'

'No-one knows where I am except Harriet and she won't tell anyone,' said Nicole. 'But I can't bear to look at Daniel because he reminds me of Bradley. It's so unfair but I can't help it.' She gazed unhappily down at the cup in her hand.

'I'll tell him to clear off early tomorrow morning, just see if I don't.'

Nicole laughed shakily, trying to imagine a fierce Zelda doing just that instead of smothering him with loving kindness.

'Zelda, you're a saint,' she said. 'And you've got your own troubles I haven't even asked about.'

'All behind me now.' She glanced down at her wrist in plaster. 'Well, almost.'

'Good for you.'

Zelda waved her good hand. 'This room's all right now and the two bedrooms.' Her smile faded. 'But I need to get the catering side sorted out or I'll be in trouble.'

Nicole sat upright and put her empty cup

down on the tray. 'But I'm here to help you do that. Lead on, Zelda, and show me what needs doing. Together we'll have the place up and running in no time.'

Zelda's eyes brightened. 'You want to see it now?'

'Why not?'

The phone rang. Nicole sank back into her cushions.

'That'll be Mark,' said Zelda as she got up to reach across to the small table by the window to answer it.

'Harriet?' Nicole heard her say in surprise. 'How nice to hear from you, dear. Are you keeping well and that husband of yours looking after you? Nicole? Oh yes, she's here, safe and well. You'd better talk to her yourself.'

Nicole took the receiver from her, ashamed of being so full of her own concerns that she had forgotten to phone her sister as soon as she got here. Now she hastily apologised and promised to keep in touch.

'And she really doesn't know anything about that horrible chap?' Zelda said as she replaced the receiver.

Nicole shook her head. 'I thought it best not to tell her in the circumstances.'

'You'll be all right here, my love,' Zelda said with confidence.

*   *   *

21

Later, Nicole got ready for bed in the room downstairs that her aunt had so lovingly set out as her tearoom. It must have looked attractive before those thugs got going on it. The curtains had been ripped from the rails, china smashed and tables and chairs broken. She had gazed at the damaged room in silence, imagining it as it had once been.

'Mark said to leave this for the time being and get my living space sorted out first,' Zelda said. 'I wish now we'd started here and left the rest.'

A bad mark for Mark, Nicole thought. But he may have had a point.

'The curtains are ruined,' said Zelda. 'But Pippa's promised me some she wove herself. Kind of her, I think. She's the girl next door. A bit scatty but a heart of gold.'

'And you're afraid the curtains will be clumsy, woven from seaweed from the beach in dreary colours that'll put your customers off their food?'

Zelda laughed. 'Hark at me when she's being so generous. But you know me too well, my love. Pessimistic to the core.'

'You're anything but that,' Nicole said with feeling. Zelda was so cheerful in the face of her troubles that for a brief spell she had forgotten her own concerns as they discussed the work ahead.

Before getting into bed she pulled the

22

curtains a little apart and gazed out across the moonlit garden and the rough land beyond to the sea in the distance. The high rocky outcrop that Daniel had called the Dancing Hole looked dark against the shimmering water. The tent wasn't visible from here but he would have pitched it in the most sheltered spot. She hoped he'd be off early next day so that she'd never see him again.

MEETING DANIEL AGAIN

The sun had barely risen next morning when Nicole sprang out of bed and rushed across to the window to draw the curtains aside. The murmuring sea looked darkly mysterious at this hour but already sunshine was touching the tips of the rocks on the headland.

She watched the light gradually ripple over land and water and the seagulls winging their way out to sea. Nearer at hand a robin perched on the back of a garden seat and cocked his head to one side as if considering what to do next.

She got herself ready to go downstairs, eager to check that Daniel had kept his word.

To her surprise Zelda was already in the kitchen standing at the stove with her back to her. There was something about the stoop to her shoulders that made Nicole pause in concern. 'Zelda?'

Her aunt turned and immediately her face lit up into a radiant smile. 'I was going to bring a cup of tea up to you, Nicole dear.'

'You're OK, Zelda?'

'And why shouldn't I be this lovely shining morning?'

No reason at all apart from delayed shock at the break-in and a broken wrist, Nicole thought. It seemed that she was needed here more than she realised and was doubly glad she had come.

The small table in the kitchen area was laid with mugs, bowls and spoons and on the side was a freshly baked batch of scones.

Nicole looked at them in astonishment. 'How did you manage those with only one hand?'

Zelda, making porridge, laughed. 'I won't be beaten, you know, dear. I managed.'

'I don't see how.'

Zelda waved a dripping spoon. 'Porridge?'

'How could I refuse? I'm simply starving.'

'You look perky this morning, dear. Sit down and get this into you.'

'Aren't you going to have some too?'

'Presently perhaps.'

'But you'll sit down with me and have something?' said Nicole. 'I need to hear the plans for the day. I want to be made full use of, you know.' If Zelda could cope with her troubles without complaint then so could she,

24

she thought, humbled.

'I'll make coffee first.' Zelda filled two cups from the cafetiere and carried each with care to the table. 'Milk? I've already had a look outside. No sign of the tent. Your young friend must have got off early.'

Nicole added milk to her coffee and passed the jug to Zelda. Then she poured a little on her porridge and helped herself to golden syrup. She ate in silence.

By now he would be striding away along the coast path, covering the miles swiftly with those long legs of his.

'More, dear?' Zelda asked as Nicole scraped the last of the porridge round her bowl.

Suddenly Nicole was no longer hungry. She shook her head. 'I can't wait to get started on the tearoom.'

'Me neither,' said Zelda. She flicked an orange scarf off the back of her chair and wound it round her neck. 'There, let's go.'

Nicole could see that the first job was to clear the room and stack all the broken furniture, the ruined straw matting and other bits and pieces outside. Under Zelda's supervision she carried, pushed and heaved until it was all done.

'Mark and Olaf between them got the dresser back in its position against the wall yesterday morning,' Zelda said. 'But we didn't have time for more.'

'Because of going to the Cash-and-Carry?'

said Nicole.

Zelda nodded. 'It had to be done, dear. Laurie would have taken me if he'd been at home, Laurie Williams, Olaf and Pippa's father, but he's away for a week or two so Mark took me instead. Mark's been so kind. They all have, he and Olaf and Pippa.'

'I'll bet you've been kind to them in the past.'

'I hope so, dear,' said Zelda. 'But I owe them a huge debt.'

She looked so woebegone that Nicole resolved to find some way of repaying them in return for helping her aunt.

'And now it's going to be a lovely day,' Zelda said, smiling again.

'I'll check the garden furniture and see if it needs wiping down,' Nicole said.

She tackled the chairs first and then the tables. Her cloth was soaked in seconds, but the sunshine would complete the job before anyone wanted to use them. She stood for a moment, a gentle salty breeze on her face. In the distance a tractor started up and she heard the lowing of cattle. The robin she had seen earlier came hopping nearby. 'Lucky you, having all this to enjoy,' she told it, smiling. And she was lucky, too, and so was Zelda having such good friends.

Back in the cleared tearoom she plugged in the vacuum cleaner. 'While you're doing that I'll make sure the kitchen's tidy,' said Zelda.

'And you'll take a look in the mirror too?' said Nicole, smiling.

Zelda's left hand flew to her face. 'Like that is it? Naughty girl not to tell me.'

'I expect I'm as bad.'

'You'd look attractive in any circumstances, dear, especially now you've got some colour in your cheeks.'

Nicole smiled. 'Don't give me that. Now get going on with the coffee before the clamouring hordes arrive.'

She worked hard, emptying the dust bag from the vacuum cleaner several times. Then she filled a bucket with soapy water and got down to scrubbing the bare floor boards. The work was deeply satisfying as the area of wet floor increased. After a while she sat back on her heels to admire it. Honest hard work never killed anyone, she thought. In fact it often did a power of good.

She heard the sound of a vehicle pulling up outside and then voices. This could be customers turning up for coffee and some of those delicious-looking scones. A glimmer of excitement ran through her. She sprang up, her mouth watering.

The floor near where she stood was beginning to dry and she crept across to the window to check if the garden chairs were occupied. But no, there they were, dry now but empty. There were sounds of heavy movement, scraping and thumping as if someone was loading a vehicle with an awkward cargo.

And that's what it was, of course, the damaged furniture being removed from where she had dumped it not so long before. Someone was quick to take action.

The vehicle started up and was off. Moments later Zelda appeared in the doorway with her orange scarf in her hand and her wavy hair loose about her face, looking a lot happier now.

'Finished in here? Good girl. All the rubbish has gone and we can start afresh. We got some good bargains on tables and chairs at the furniture recycling place near Penzance yesterday. They've just told me they're going to deliver this afternoon.'

'I'd better get cleaned up after I've emptied this lot,' Nicole said.

'I'll do that, dear. Off you go!'

Nicole's spirits lifted at the scent of freshly ground coffee wafting up to her as she came downstairs after a quick shower.

'We'll take it outside,' Zelda called. 'We'll use up some of these scones.'

'And eat up the profits?'

'I'll make some more,' Zelda promised.

But that wasn't so easy with only one hand, Nicole thought. She wished she had Zelda's skill but she was willing to learn.

Seated at one of the wooden garden tables with the sunshine full on her face she felt more relaxed than she had done for months, even though she sensed that something was troubling her aunt.

'People might still think the place is closed,' Zelda said. 'I'll have to get that damaged notice board back up for this side of the cottage.'

'They'll see us,' Nicole said. 'They'll think we're happy customers.'

She looked across to the coast path in the distance as it wound its way past the headland. She hadn't seen any walkers this morning but then she hadn't been looking. There were certainly none now.

Zelda frowned and Nicole looked at her anxiously. Her aunt's normal optimism had taken a surprising downturn. 'It's early in the day yet,' she said consolingly. 'Not much past eleven. They'll come. And if they don't I'll go about with a huge fishing net and rake them in.'

'Hi there!' called a voice from somewhere nearby.

Zelda looked pleased. 'Pippa! Come and join us.'

Pippa, the girl from next door, came round the corner with her arms full of colourful fabric and an anxious expression on her face. 'I can't stop,' she said. 'We've heard reports that a diver's been spotted down the coast caught up in fishing net and Olaf's keen to check on what's going on.'

'A diver?' said Nicole in alarm.

29

'Great Northern Diver,' said Pippa, giving her a brief smile. 'One of the UK's largest diving birds.'

'Oh, I see.'

'They're usually only seen off the Scottish coastline in winter but sometimes one shows up here. And now this one's got itself in trouble.'

Zelda was fingering the curtains that Pippa had dumped on an empty chair. 'But these are lovely, dear.'

'Olaf wants to get off at once,' Pippa said. She stood poised, looking from one to the other, her long skirt swishing the grass.

'You're such a clever girl, dear,' said Zelda.

Pippa shrugged. 'I thought I'd drop these in for you now, Zelda, before we go. Fancy coming with us, either of you? We've got room in the van.'

Zelda's eyes were alight with enthusiasm. 'Do go with them, Nicole dear. It will be lovely for you. Olaf's a bit of a birdwatcher and you could learn a lot from him.'

'But . . .' Nicole hesitated.

'I have to be here for seeing the furniture in,' said Zelda.

'Do come,' said Pippa, smiling at Nicole. 'Olaf'll be pleased. He likes talking about birds and I take it you don't know a lot about them?'

'Not much,' Nicole admitted. Bird-watching was the last thing on her mind at the moment but she would go if it pleased Zelda.

Olaf might be good at imparting information, but his social skills left much to be desired, Nicole found.

He frowned on seeing her. 'We're wasting time.'

'You can tell Nicole all about it as we go along,' said Pippa. She opened the front passenger door of the van that was already parked outside their cottage.

'Get in then,' Olaf ordered.

Nicole hurried to climb into the back and fastened her seatbelt. She gazed at the back of Olaf's dark head as they set off. His hair was thick and wavy and strands of it had caught inside the collar of his T-shirt.

'I don't know how they'll manage to extricate that diver,' Olaf said. He sounded friendlier now. 'They're strong, those birds. If there's any life left in it there'll be a fine old struggle.'

'But there's some hope?' said Nicole.

'I'm not at all sure there'll be a successful outcome.'

There wasn't anything anyone could say to that and Pippa, sunk low in her seat, remained silent. Nicole wondered who had discovered the bird and how news about its predicament had travelled so quickly.

They reached the village and turned right

31

onto the narrow and twisting main road. Dark clouds hid the sun now and the grey stone houses looked gloomy.

They seemed to be going for miles, but at last Olaf turned off to the right and they trundled down an even narrower lane. Ahead of them Nicole saw a steep grass-covered headland.

Olaf pulled into a field where other vehicles were parked, including an RSPB van.

'Cape Witten,' Pippa said. 'We often come here beachcombing for our supplies.'

Supplies of what, Nicole wondered? Sand from the small beach in its rocky cove, grass from the headland? There seemed little else.

'Driftwood,' Pippa explained as if she had spoken. 'Useful things like that.'

They got out. Olaf slammed his door shut with a resounding crash and strode off towards the higher ground of the headland with his binoculars slung round his neck.

'He's worried,' Pippa said, following him anxiously with her eyes.

'Don't you want to go with him?'

'He's best on his own.' With a wave of her hand Pippa indicated the beach where a crowd of people were gathered. Some had binoculars to their eyes and others had cameras at the ready. Someone with a video camera swung it in a wide arc before focussing on a small boat some way offshore.

With her sandals in her hand Nicole

followed Pippa to the water's edge, sharply aware of the tension that was in the air.

'They're having trouble,' someone said. 'That bird's got enough movement and wingspan to duck every time they try a rescue attempt. They've been at it for hours already ever since that young lad raised the alarm at daybreak.'

Nicole imagined the bird's terror as it struggled in vain. It seemed a futile exercise to try to free it when it was determined to do it without help. But what did she know?

She glanced at Pippa standing motionless at her side in her long floaty skirt and ruffled blouse. The girl's face looked troubled. 'I wouldn't want a lot of interference if I was caught in a net,' she murmured.

Nicole couldn't help a snort of laughter as she imagined the scene and then was instantly ashamed. This was serious business.

Pippa turned to her, half-smiling. 'Are you bored with all this?'

Nicole hastened to reassure her. 'I'm sorry for the poor bird,' she said. 'I wish I could help. But can anyone really do anything?'

'They have to try,' said Pippa simply.

'Because a Great Northern Diver's rare in these parts?'

'Because it needs help.'

Nicole nodded. They were good people, Pippa and Olaf. She felt humbled and ashamed of her cynical words when to them it

33

mattered so much.

After a while most of the spectators began to disperse. Nicole saw that the two men in the boat seemed to have given up their attempt to free the netted bird and were heading away towards the headland.

'That's that, then,' said Pippa. She sounded uncaring but Nicole suspected that she was deeply saddened.

Olaf, too, as he came striding down from his vantage point, seemed to accept the decision to leave the bird alone and to put the failure out of his mind, but must have minded desperately too.

He placed his binoculars inside their case and turned to the young man in shorts walking at his side.

Nicole let out a startled gasp as she saw who he was.

Daniel didn't appear aware of her as he listened to what Olaf was saying but she thought she saw a faint flush on his cheeks.

A smile lit up Olaf's features as they reached the girls. 'My sister, Pippa,' he said with pride. 'And Pippa, this is Daniel Murray. Remember his article on the re-introduction of the red kite in south west Scotland you found so interesting? He's done useful work here already in alerting the RSPB.'

Pippa stepped forward and took his hand. 'A friend indeed.' She gazed up into his face with such admiration that Nicole felt uncomfortable.

'Olaf's been telling me something of your work,' Daniel said, smiling down at Pippa. 'It sounds truly fascinating. And you're both passionate about birds, too.'

'Especially Olaf,' Pippa said. 'He'd like to be caring for them full time.' She picked up a piece of knotted driftwood and looked at it dreamily.

'I'm not prepared to let Daniel leave us and go on his way that easily,' said Olaf. 'He knows a thing or two about the wildlife centre up the coast. I'd rather like to pick his brains. What do you say, Pippa?'

'Of course not,' said Pippa, looking shocked at the idea.

Nicole moved a little away from the others as if by distancing herself she could make herself invisible as indeed she felt she was. Why had she got herself into this when it would have been so simple to have thanked Pippa for her invitation to accompany them on what had turned out to be a waste of time? She could have then declined with the perfect excuse that she was at Kenvarloe to help Zelda and need never have come face to face with Daniel Murray again.

'And this is Nicole,' Pippa said hurriedly as if she had nearly forgotten. 'We brought her with us.'

Daniel inclined his head. 'We've met already when I pitched my tent near her aunt's cottage last night. Hello, Nicole.'

'So that was your tent?' said Olaf. 'We live in the cottage next door. What a pity we didn't know.'

Daniel smiled. 'I'm sorry, too. A good discussion on local birds and life in general would have made a good end to the day.'

Nicole felt herself flush. 'You left very early this morning,' she said, an edge to her voice.

'It seemed best in the circumstances.'

She looked at him quickly and then away again. She wondered that someone didn't pick up on the meaning behind his words.

'You wouldn't have noticed the diver in trouble if you hadn't,' Pippa said.

'True.'

And much good it did it, Nicole thought, and then was ashamed of her unfriendly thoughts.

There was something about Daniel Murray that brought out the worst in her.

NICOLE SETTLES IN

Pippa still held the piece of misshapen wood she had picked up from the beach. 'Definitely useful,' she said.

Olaf looked at it in approval, his long thin face lit up by his smile. 'I can do something with that. We'll take a load of that back if there's more where it came from.'

'There's plenty,' said Pippa. She glanced along the beach to where a line of jagged rocks stuck out into the sea. 'Mark's been out fishing,' she said. 'He's coming back this way now.'

Nicole looked too and saw a boat heading towards them.

'We'll get a fire going with anything that's no use to us,' Olaf said. 'Come on, everyone, get cracking. We've brought cooking things. I'll get them from the van.'

Nicole set to work with the others gathering pieces of wood washed up by the tide as if this was the most natural thing in the world. She felt as if she were in a dream and at any moment would wake up and wonder what she was doing here among strangers when she should have been back at Kenvarloe helping Zelda.

Daniel was keeping well away from her, she noticed. Every now and again he and Pippa paused to show one another what they had discovered lurking on the sand, their heads close together.

Nicole turned her back to them and concentrated on the job in hand, feeling strangely left out.

By the time the boat reached the shore, Olaf was back and had got the fire going with small pieces of wood and dried brown seaweed that smelt of salt and hissed as the flames licked it.

To Nicole's surprise he added larger pieces of wood from a pile that looked to her eyes much the better ones because they were smooth and straight.

Soon the fire was blazing merrily. She moved back, feeling the sudden heat as sparks flew up into the air.

The man in the boat reached the beach. He clambered out, pulled the boat up onto the soft sand well away from the water's edge. Then he leaned inside to heave out a bucket and carried it up the beach towards them.

'Mackerel,' he said. 'Any good?'

'Brilliant,' said Pippa. 'We've got bread and cooking things. You've been missing a lot of action, Mark. You should have been here.'

'I was well out of it,' he said quietly. 'You know my views.'

It seemed they did, Nicole thought, because they let the subject drop.

'You'll join us, Mark?' asked Olaf.

He shook his head. 'Not this time. Zelda needs help this afternoon. I'd better be on my way back.'

'Me too,' said Nicole. 'I promised to be there.'

He turned to her and smiled. His grey hair was cut short. He looked kind and unthreatening in his pale blue shirt, the sort of man who disliked pushing himself forward.

'You know Zelda?' he said.

'I'm Nicole Leavey. Zelda's my aunt. I

arrived yesterday to help out.'

'I'll drive you,' he said. 'My car's over there.'

She hesitated as she saw Daniel looking at her. Was he expecting her to come out with something as scathing as she had to him yesterday? She took a deep breath. 'That would be kind,' she said.

'We'll leave this rabble to play campfires then, shall we?'

Olaf looked apologetic. 'We need to get some info on a few things,' he said. 'If you're there to help instead, Mark, Zelda won't mind if we don't show up, will she?'

'Fine by me,' said Mark.

Pippa indicated the pile of misshapen driftwood that Olaf had considered too good to burn. 'There's all that to load into the van, you see, and it'll take time,' she said.

'I'll give you a hand,' said Daniel.

Already he had gutted a couple of mackerel and thrown the insides into the fire. The smell followed Nicole and Mark as they headed for his Volvo in the car park.

'I know Olaf and Pippa of old,' he said. 'They'll be there for hours yet. No understanding of time, either of them.'

'They seem so relaxed and laid-back,' said Nicole rather enviously.

'Too much so sometimes. Olaf would be better employed looking after that gallery of theirs than thinking about birds. They need someone to light a fuse behind them and make

39

them see sense.'

Mark opened the passenger door for her and she got in. He slipped into the driving seat and put the car into gear.

'They have a gallery?' said Nicole in surprise as they set off

'Their father pays the rent of the place for them, I believe. He thinks they're wasting their time but is prepared to go along with it for the time being.'

'Good for them,' said Nicole.

'You believe in following one's dreams?'

'Of course. Isn't that what Zelda's doing?'

He nodded thoughtfully. 'You've got me there.'

Nicole smiled. In Mark's pleasant undemanding company the drive home was enjoyable and seemed to take no time at all. It was a smooth ride, too, compared with the van. He was easy to talk to, asking one or two questions and listening with interest to Nicole's replies about being glad to do what she could to help her aunt get her business back together again.

'That break-in shook her up more than she admits,' he said. 'And then to have that accident. It was good that Olaf was at hand at the time and knew what to do in that quiet way of his. He's a good lad.

'They deserve to have a bit of success in their business even if they set about things in rather a haphazard way. I'm fond of them

40

both.'

'Have the police got any leads on the break-in and who did it?' Nicole asked.

'Not as far as I know. Zelda doesn't like to talk about it.'

'D'you think they'll come back?'

Mark shook his head. 'The police think it was a one-off, young yobbos getting a kick out of trashing the place. Luckily they didn't want catering equipment.'

'So they're not planning to set up in opposition?'

Mark's slow smile was attractive and suited his rather subdued personality, she thought. He seemed a pleasant uncomplicated sort of man and she wondered what part he played in Zelda's life.

'So you keep your boat at Witten?' she said as they turned off the main road by the church and set off down the track to the cottages.

'I borrow it occasionally from a friend when I feel like a spot of fishing,' he said. 'It makes a fine day out but I haven't yet persuaded your aunt to come with me.'

Hearing the car, Zelda came out to greet them. 'Any luck with freeing the poor bird?'

'Afraid not,' said Nicole.' They tried their best though but it didn't want any help.'

'That's so sad. And you left Olaf and Pippa down there?'

Mark smiled. 'Not on purpose, Zelda, I assure you. Nicole will bear me out. I'm going to be Olaf this afternoon and do your furniture moving for you, with Nicole's help.'

Zelda looked pleased. She glanced at her watch. 'It's due in half-an-hour.'

'Perfect,' said Mark.

'Have you eaten? Sandwiches only, I'm afraid.' Her smile faded. 'Some people came earlier but they didn't stop.'

'Their loss, our gain,' said Mark. 'Don't worry about it.'

They sat outside on the patio looking out to the sea. A perfect spot, Nicole thought. She felt the peace seeping into her and she closed her eyes for a moment glorying in her surroundings.

The furniture arrived as soon as they had eaten. With Mark and Nicole's help the unloading was accomplished quickly and it was all soon in place in the tearoom.

Zelda stood in the doorway, her head a little to one side as she inspected her purchases. 'Not bad,' she said. 'Just let me get my checked cloths on the tables and some vases of flowers.'

'Some of the yellow broom?' said Nicole. 'Shall I do it for you?'

Zelda looked horrified. 'And have all the piskies of Cornwall clamouring round to see who could do us most harm?'

'Is it unlucky to bring it indoors?'

'You could say that, if you were as superstitious as Zelda,' Mark said, the side of his mouth twitching.

42

Nicole smiled back at him. 'I won't risk it. I'll find something else instead.'

'The little glass pots I use are under the sink, dear,' said Zelda.

Nicole could hear the gentle murmur of the sea in the distance when she went outside and wandered happily up the track picking scabious and wild thyme. The blue and mauve looked good, she thought when she had picked enough. Surely there was nothing here that Zelda might object to?

*   *   *

Pippa and Olaf were back by late afternoon, bringing with them the vanload of misshapen wood and the remaining mackerel that Mark had given them.

Zelda received it with delight. 'We'll have a barbecue, shall we? What do you say, Nicole? It's a lovely evening. What a pity Mark's gone.'

'I'd offer to cook the fish for you immediately on that barbecue of yours if we hadn't to off-load this lot,' Olaf said.

'No need, dear. You're our guests this evening, you and Pippa.'

Pippa looked doubtful for a moment but then smiled. 'It's lucky we both like barbecued mackerel.'

'We'll have a party,' said Zelda, eyes shining. 'A welcome-to-Nicole party. I'll phone Mark at once and see if he's free. Now, where

43

did I put my supplies of charcoal?'

*　　　*　　　*

Later, with the charcoal a white-hot glow and the filleted fish sizzling on the grill, Zelda looked round happily at her guests. Pippa was wearing another long floaty skirt, this time of bright orange and red. Both Mark and Olaf were in shorts and T-shirts.

Pippa had arrived carrying something in a paper bag, holding it as if it was precious. She presented it to Zelda with a smile.

'For me?' said Zelda, flushing with pleasure.

'For the tearoom wall,' Pippa said shyly. 'We thought it might look good there. Olaf made it when we got back.'

Nicole opened the bag for Zelda and revealed a boat made out of driftwood on a background of scuffed blue. The sails were a delicate shade of lemon yellow. She saw at once that though the picture was of simple construction, Olaf's imagination had made it into a charming object.

'It's beautiful,' said Zelda, rubbing the fingers of her left hand over the rough wood of the boat. She looked as if she couldn't bear to let Mark take it from her to place safely in its bag.

'Best to keep it away from the cooking,' he said. 'I'll take it inside for you.'

Nicole stood at a table placed closer to the

44

barbecue to act as a serving space. She looked across at their guests who were now helping themselves liberally from the jug of fruit punch. Pippa filled a glass for her and placed it nearby.

Nicole smiled her thanks. It was incredible that already they felt like old friends.

Piles of granary rolls on a wooden platter were ready to be filled with the grilled mackerel. 'So much easier to eat like that without knives and forks,' Zelda said. 'Especially for me. And it doesn't matter, does it? We can help ourselves from the bowls of tomatoes and green salad with our fingers. Save on the washing up.'

Nicole agreed, her mouth watering. A simple meal but an appetising one, she thought. And what better place to enjoy it on this lovely calm evening among friends? This was worlds away from her busy life in London.

The sun, an hour lower in the sky now than when Zelda had invited Olaf and Pippa to join them, shone full on the damaged notice board that Mark had placed temporarily in its old position facing the sea, promising to repair it properly when he had time. In this light the damage wasn't obvious. A good omen, Nicole wondered? She hoped so. Zelda deserved some good fortune.

She glanced towards the rocky headland silhouetted against the sky and the delicate pink light on the sea. It looked magical.

45

Several late walkers were coming along the coast path now. They stopped to admire the view of distant headlands to the south, the most prominent one Witten Head. Then they left the coast path, heading inland. Could they be coming here, enticed by the notice board? It seemed like it.

'I think we've got visitors,' she warned.

Zelda paused, holding her spatula aloft. 'Coming here?'

'Looks like it.'

The group of walkers appeared round the side of the cottage. 'Oh good, you're open for business?' one of them said with pleasure.

Her companions looked at Zelda hopefully. 'That lovely smell. We simply couldn't resist it.'

Nicole sprang up at once. 'Of course we're open for business. You're welcome. Fresh mackerel's on the menu tonight in homemade granary rolls with as much salad as you can eat. The fish was caught just a few hours ago down the coast not far from here. Isn't that so, Zelda?'

Bemused, Zelda nodded and then beamed round at everybody among the bustle of seats being found. Nicole hastily collected a few extra chairs from indoors and then seized the salad bowl to replenish it from fresh supplies in the kitchen. She knew there were plenty more rolls that could soon be defrosted. Mark followed her and piled a bowl with the surplus

46

mackerel he'd filleted earlier ready for the freezer.

Out at the barbecue Zelda turned the pieces of mackerel on the grill and the aromatic smell rose in the evening air as the talk became lively.

To Nicole's surprise Pippa, suddenly animated, was at Zelda's side. 'Please let me do something,' she said.

She was surprisingly helpful, flitting from table to table handing round the plates of mackerel rolls. Her eyes sparkled and her cheeks were faintly flushed as she checked that everyone had what they wanted.

'Please, don't move,' she said to one of the older men who seemed about to struggle up from his seat.

In an instant she had carried the salad bowl to his table, waited until he had helped himself and then replaced it.

She sat down at her place next to Olaf but Nicole could see that all the time she was eating her eyes darted from guest to guest, checking they were happy. Then she was up again, collecting empty plates.

Nicole got up too. Pippa, seeing she was taking her pile back to the kitchen, followed her.

'You like doing this sort of thing?' Nicole asked with interest.

'You're so lucky,' Pippa breathed. She placed her pile of plates on the draining board.

'What about the washing up?'

Nicole smiled. 'Don't worry. I'll do it later. You're a guest. And you're lucky, too, Pippa, living in a place like Kenvarloe.'

Pippa's eyes shone. 'And helping Olaf with his work.'

'What exactly does he do?'

'He makes things out of finds from the beach, driftwood and things that get washed up by the sea. Then we sell them.'

'So that's why you wanted so many misshapen pieces of wood?'

'He sees things in the interesting shapes that other people don't.'

'It sounds fascinating.'

'We've got this gallery we've called *Flotsam Follies* in Trevillick. You must come and see for yourself, Nicole.'

'I'd love to.'

Nicole smiled as they went to join the others outside. Maybe she was becoming cured of her anxiety about Bradley already because until now she hadn't thought of him once this evening. In fact she would hardly even remember what he looked like if Daniel hadn't been around. All she needed was time and, hopefully, that was what she would be getting here in Kenvarloe.

ANOTHER MEETING WITH DANIEL

Afterwards, when Olaf and Pippa had returned to their cottage and the three of them were in the kitchen clearing up, Zelda flopped down on the stool by the door.

'I simply can't believe it,' she said. 'Seven customers and all of them pleased with such a simple meal.'

'More than pleased,' said Nicole. 'You were a star turn with the frying pan. Zelda, the one-armed chef. You were a sensation.'

Mark smiled at her. 'If this goes on I can see I'll have to get myself out there fishing all the time instead of tending my market garden.'

'Ah, but we'll be relying on you to keep us supplied with fresh salad things,' said Zelda. 'All local produce, you see. It could be the start of something big.'

'I certainly hope so for your sake, Zelda my dear,' Mark said with feeling.

Somehow everything seemed possible in this euphoric moment, Nicole thought. 'And what about Pippa?' she said. 'Has she done waitressing before? If not, she's a natural.'

'She's got hidden talents, that girl,' said Zelda. 'I was as surprised as you, dear. And did our guests really order a similar mackerel meal for sixteen next Saturday or was I dreaming?'

Nicole smiled. 'We'll have time to get organised.'

'But I can't just give them grilled mackerel in a roll,' said Zelda.

'Why not, if that's what they want?' said Mark. 'You have to please your customers and I think they were well pleased this evening.'

Zelda sat up straight with a glow about her at the sudden change of fortune. 'We've got a good stock of flour and yeast in for the rolls and I'll get stuck in with the baking tomorrow to stock the freezer,' she said. 'How much mackerel have we got left? I'll gladly purchase all you can supply, Mark.'

'Glad to be of use,' he said quietly.

Zelda looked up and Nicole saw their eyes meet for a long illuminating moment. She felt suddenly in the way.

When Mark had gone Nicole stacked the plates she had just dried into a neat pile at one side of the worktop. So Mark was a market gardener? Her lips twitched as she remembered guessing this yesterday with only the small hydrangea plants in the bed outside as possible evidence. He was a fisherman, too, in a small way. Or maybe a bigger way now if this mackerel idea caught on.

Zelda got up. 'We've done enough for tonight, dear. I'll leave the rest till the morning.'

Nicole yawned, exhaustion finally getting to her. All she wanted now was to take another shower to rid herself of any lingering fishy smell and then get into bed and fall immediately asleep.

*   *   *

She woke during the night and heard the sound of rain pattering on the window. She got out of bed to investigate and stared out for a moment into the invisible darkness. She thought of what Pippa had told her earlier about Olaf knowing from the first moment what he could make from each piece of driftwood they found on the beach. The inspiration came from the wood itself, she had said.

Now, Nicole wondered at the life these two had chosen for themselves. It seemed incredible to her, from her busy city background, that two such people would choose to live a hand-to-mouth existence in the west of Cornwall creating beautiful things from twisted wood that others might think fit only for the bonfire.

But that was Cornwall for you, she thought. That would be Harriet's reaction. West Barbary, a wild barbaric place. There must be some sort of magic in the air that wiped all sensible thoughts from your mind. She hadn't thought of those messages on her mobile since turning up here. Maybe putting bad things behind you was the sensible thing to do.

51

She went back to bed. The wind was getting up now. She lay listening to it whistling round the cottage and thought of Daniel Murray camping somewhere down the coast in his flimsy tent. Neither Pippa nor Olaf had mentioned him this evening and she wondered why they had wanted to talk more to him earlier on Witten beach.

Drowsily she thought about it until at last she fell asleep again.

The next time she woke daylight filled the room. There was no drumming of rain on the window now and the wind had dropped.

*   *   *

There was plenty to do in the next few days. Mark went fishing again and Nicole spent hours filleting and cleaning the mackerel he caught. Zelda's job was to pack the fillets for the freezer into containers. Both were glad when the messy job was done.

'The freezer's bulging,' Zelda said, rinsing her hand in the sink.

'That's what I like to hear,' said Nicole sitting down at the table. 'All we need now is a glorious sunny evening on Saturday so the group can enjoy eating outside. Can you imagine them all in the tearoom, the place steamed up and Pippa's lovely new curtains stinking of mackerel?'

Zelda shuddered as she reached for the

hand towel and began rubbing her hands dry. 'Perhaps it wasn't such a good idea after all, dear. Teas and lunches are one thing but evening meals are another.'

'But it's a simple menu,' Nicole reminded her. 'What can go wrong?'

Zelda glanced at the window. 'Need I say?'

Nicole laughed. 'Of course it's a good idea, Zelda, whatever the weather. Brilliant in fact. Morning coffee, light lunches, cream teas, mackerel dinners. We'll be rushed off our feet.'

Zelda's sudden smile lit up her face. 'Of course, dear, you're so right. I don't know what I'd do without you. Enough of my dreary talk. Those rolls will be ready for baking now.'

Nicole sprang up. 'I'll get them.'

The two trays of jumbo-sized bread rolls had been set to rise out of the way in the tearoom. She paused on the threshold and studied the room critically. They had done a good job in the last few days. The pretty curtains Pippa had made hung at the latticed windows. The tables were set out with cutlery on the checked cloths and the vases of thyme and scabious looked charming.

She sniffed appreciatively at the sweet scent of wild honeysuckle that wafted across from the extra vase she had placed on the dresser. The replacement china looked good on it too. Most of it was white edged with green that Pippa had found for them in the St Benedict charity shop in town.

She carried the trays of rolls into the kitchen where the oven was ready for them. Soon the smell of baking bread filled the kitchen.

'Better than mackerel,' said Olaf from the open doorway.

Zelda laughed. 'You've not come scrounging?'

'Do I ever?'

Nicole smiled. Olaf seemed a different person today and far more approachable. Gone was the worried frown. His torn jeans had been replaced by smarter ones and his white T-shirt looked new.

'Off somewhere nice?' asked Zelda.

'Pippa thinks we should open up the gallery today. She wants to know if she can get you anything from town.'

'I don't think so, dear,' said Zelda. 'Only a vanload of lunch customers.'

Olaf looked solemn. 'We'll do our best.'

'They'll even do that, I shouldn't wonder,' said Zelda when he had gone. 'Their laid-back lifestyle often has strange results.'

The telephone rang. Zelda reached for the receiver. 'For you,' she said holding it out to Nicole.

With reluctance Nicole took it from her and held it to her ear.

'Something wrong?' asked Zelda in concern.

Nicole replaced the receiver. 'My mobile's ready for collection. It's fine. No problem.'

'But that's good, dear, isn't it?'

'Well, yes.' Nicole tried to sound positive but now she would find out if there was another message from Bradley on it.

'I wonder if Olaf and Pippa have left yet and would give you a lift?' Zelda said and was off at once without waiting to hear whether or not Nicole thought it a good idea. Minutes later she was back.

'You're in luck, dear. They're just off. Hurry now. Where's your bag? Here take mine. You can pay me back later if you need to.'

Her aunt's kindness was sometimes misplaced, Nicole thought as she slammed the van door and they drove off. Here she was, clutching a strange bag without time even to think of getting her jacket when she would have liked time to think about this and to decide what to do for the best. Maybe it would have been good to leave her mobile where it was for a day or two. But that was cowardice. She had to collect it sometime.

Olaf was pulling in to the side at the top of the hill now that led down to the town. 'Our usual place,' he said as he opened the door for her. 'A bit of a walk, but we can stay parked here as long as we like.'

'Or as little,' said Pippa, smiling. 'We like to keep our options open.'

Nicole was more than happy to walk down the steep hill to the busy harbour with the squawking gulls wheeling overhead. Beyond

55

it the sea was brilliant blue and over the other side of the bay some white-sailed dinghies were setting out from shore. She wished she could appreciate it properly, but the thought of another message from Bradley on her mobile was like a dead weight. Next time she came to Trevillick she would bring her camera.

'Would you like to see our gallery, Nicole?' Pippa asked when they had negotiated the narrow winding street and had arrived at the bottom among the crowds of holidaymakers. 'Then you'll know where it is when you've finished your shopping. We needn't be too long if you're in a hurry to get back.'

'I can't do that. This is your work, your livelihood.'

'No matter,' said Olaf. 'One of us can remain here fighting off the hordes of customers while the other drives you home.'

Pippa laughed. 'I wish.'

'No way,' said Nicole firmly. 'I'll get the bus.'

'We'll see,' said Olaf. 'Along here.'

He led the way down another narrow cobbled street, getting the key out of the pocket of his jeans as they walked. Halfway along he stopped and looked proudly up at a board swinging from above the window. On it Nicole saw the name *Flotsam Follies* painted in flaked white and gold paint on a green board.

Inside, Nicole stared at the pictures made from beach finds that hung on the walls and

56

then looked more closely at them, marvelling at Olaf's skill.

'They've definitely got something about them out of the ordinary, Olaf,' she said. She moved across the uneven floor to a table made from driftwood displaying all sorts of wooden ornaments. 'I can almost smell the sea and feel the breeze on my face.'

Pippa looked pleased. 'We love beach-combing, you see. Almost everything here is made from things collected on the beach.'

'And you've made all these?'

'Olaf has,' said Pippa. 'He's got a good eye.'

'I can see that,' said Nicole, impressed.

'He just sits down for a while with a piece of wood in his hand that he's found washed up with the tide and it's like the wood is telling him what to make out of it. He's good.'

Olaf looked uncomfortable. 'Not always.'

Nicole picked up a boat with striped yellow and white sails. 'They're so simple yet there's something charming about them,' she said.

'Pippa makes the sails for the boats,' said Olaf. 'And the lampshades and other things too. Some of the wood makes good lamp bases. People seem to like them.'

'I'm sure they do.'

'We were lucky to get hold of the gallery in a good position like this and so right for our purpose,' said Olaf 'A short lease it's true, but it gives us the opportunity to see if we can make a go of it. Yesterday we got the offer of some help and that's great. He'll free us to roam the beaches.'

'But where do you make all these lovely things?'

'I'll show you.' Olaf opened a door in the back wall she hadn't noticed and indicated that Nicole should follow him down some steps.

Carefully she negotiated the piles of driftwood stacked on each one. This lower room was almost the size of the one above and was filled with working tables, lathes, baskets of likely wood and rows of tools. It smelt differently too, of linseed oil and sawdust and something she couldn't define. She looked round with interest. It was definitely a working space, she thought.

In the gallery area Pippa was talking to someone. 'Our helper's arrived, Olaf,' she called.

'Daniel!' said Olaf, leaping up the steps to greet him.

Nicole's heart skipped a beat as she saw Daniel standing there in his knee-length shorts and navy sleeveless top.

He looked up and surprise flickered across his features. 'Nicole?'

She felt herself flush. 'Hi, Daniel.'

'Have you come to help too?'

'I've come into town to collect my phone,' she said awkwardly. 'I'll be off now.'

'No hurry,' said Pippa.

An anxious expression flickered across

Daniel's face. 'Ah, yes, your phone. Shall I come with you?'

'Whatever for?'

'I thought you might like company.'

'I know the way.'

Her words sounded ungracious, but they had been said now and she couldn't take them back. She moved quickly to the door and was off before anyone could stop her. She could at least have been polite, she thought. All three had offered help in one way or another and she had left without even saying goodbye. How bad-mannered was that?

Annoyed with herself, she found the little back street she had located in a hurry a few days ago on her way to Kenvarloe. She knew she was lucky to have got to them quickly after her mobile's dive into salt water and that was Daniel's doing. So why had she been so curt with him now?

Her mobile phone was as good as new, the assistant told her proudly. She thanked him and then looked at it. No new messages. She felt weak with relief.

She paid what she owed from Zelda's purse and thrust the phone into the bag, wishing she need never see it again.

PIPPA SEEMS UPSET

When Nicole and Harriet came on holidays to Trevillick as children the first thing they did was to run down to the harbour to see if the shop selling shells was still there. And it always was.

They had delighted in the baskets of tropical shells of all shapes and sizes and had taken ages to decide which ones they should buy with the money Mum and Dad gave them to last the whole week. Harriet's favourites were always the large brown spotted ones with the curly edges because they were shiny, but Nicole liked the small creamy-coloured shells with the pink centres and with a hint deep inside their crinkled exteriors that promised secrets only she could know.

She had them still, hidden away in a box in her flat at the top of her wardrobe; unlooked at for so many years. She wondered if the pink was as beautiful as she remembered it or had it faded along with so many other things that once had been precious to her.

She smiled now as she thought of their childish pleasure. She had understood the reason behind Harriet's caustic remarks about the wilds of West Cornwall only too well. She, too, had been reluctant to dwell on the pain of lost childhood happiness and had thought up many half-baked reasons for postponing her first visit to Zelda in her new home in Kenvarloe.

Now Nicole had returned to Cornwall to escape from a man so eager to pursue her that he wouldn't let her alone. She was using Cornwall because it suited her. How selfish was that?

She gave a little shiver as she walked slowly away from the phone shop. She had been anxious for nothing. Bradley had given up on her at last. Wasted emotion, she thought as she quickened her pace.

The shell shop was still there, incredible after all this time. So much had happened during those years since their parents died. From the start Zelda had taken a large part of the responsibility of looking after two teenage girls. There had been another aunt and uncle with children of their own and they had lived with them for a while, but it hadn't worked out.

The cousins hadn't liked them taking over a lot of their own space. Their parents, though kind, were always busy with something or other and finally decided to emigrate to New Zealand where Uncle Bob had family. Nicole was glad they hadn't gone too, even though they had been invited.

Inside the shell shop everything seemed smaller now as places often did on going back as an adult, she thought. Even the baskets of shells weren't as huge as she remembered them. Perhaps there wasn't as much demand for them now as in the old days. Times moved on and fashions changed.

She wished she still had the shell bracelet she had kept for years, but somehow she had mislaid it fairly recently. It was made of small cockle shells attached to a silver plated chain, not valuable, but she had liked it.

Picking up a large shell from the nearest basket, she smoothed her fingers over the surface. It felt hard and cold, but there was something deeply satisfying about the movement.

'I'll take this,' she said to the elderly assistant behind the counter who beamed back at her as she took her money and opened the till. She wrapped the chosen shell in white tissue paper.

'Do you sell many of these?' Nicole asked.

'Oh yes, m'dear, in high season. Very popular. They remind folk of the sea, I suppose, when they're a long way away from it.'

Nicole nodded. 'Like me when I was a little girl.'

She put the shell carefully in Zelda's bag and left the shop. There were still thirty minutes before the Kenvarloe bus left. Time for a quick coffee.

She found a suitable place overlooking the harbour and chose a seat outside so that she could watch the boats coming and going about their business, now that the tide was in and the expanse of golden sand between the harbour walls was fully covered. The sun glinted on the water and the brightly-painted boats looked cheerful.

She was glad she had come to Trevillick today. She needed to come back to get her memories into perspective. When she had broken her journey here on the way to Kenvarloe, there had been little time to do anything other than visit the phone shop. She had been upset, worried. Now she could relax and enjoy herself. Next time she came she would make sure to bring her camera with her.

Fourteen years was a long time to stay away from somewhere that meant so much to her. To be near Harriet in London after leaving Art College she had found a job designing birthday and Christmas cards. Then she had decided to train as a teacher. She had enjoyed her work travelling from school to school teaching art until her contract ran out at the end of the summer term.

She sipped her coffee, gazing at the cheerful scene in front of her. Then she glanced at her watch and sprang up. Missing the bus wasn't a good idea when she had been so adamant to Olaf that she didn't want a lift back to Kenvarloe.

The bus was there waiting, its running engine belting out hot smelly steam. She hurried towards it, but before she got there someone stepped in front of her. 'Hold on a minute, Nicole,' he said.

She moved back a pace. 'Daniel?'

He looked so full of confidence standing there smiling at her with the sunshine brightening his fair hair. 'Of course it's me, who else?' His voice deepened in concern and he looked at her closely. 'For goodness' sake, Nicole, what's wrong?'

She couldn't tell him. Instead she took a deep gasping breath. 'I'm all right, really, Daniel.'

'You don't look it.'

She didn't doubt that for a moment, but gave her best smile to reassure him. 'I'm sorry.'

'I don't usually have this effect on people,' he said and then added more gently, 'Come and take a seat over here for a minute or two.'

She went with him to the bench he indicated. 'I was feeling a bit shocked that's all,' she said. 'It happens sometimes.'

He sat down beside her. 'So there is something wrong?'

The bus door slid closed.

'I'm supposed to be on that,' she said as she watched it leave. But she didn't really care that it was going without her. Another would come along in an hour or so and she was in no hurry. All that mattered now was to regain her composure after the shock of thinking he was Bradley.

'Olaf sent me after you,' he said. 'You're needed at the shop. D'you think you can make it? There's something Pippa would like you to do for her.'

'There is?'

'She'll tell you. I'm going to be there for the rest of the day while they clear off to do some beachcombing. They'll drop you off at Kenvarloe on the way there.'

She stared at a seagull on the harbour wall, its beady eye on an ice cream cone held by a small boy. His mother waved it away and it took off, screaming.

'I thought you'd be miles down the coast path by now heading for Land's End,' she said.

He winced as he tried to shrug. 'I should have been, but I had a bit of an accident on some rocks at Witten. Hurt my shoulder a bit. Nothing much, but hoisting my rucksack up was not on.'

'So you've given up on your long distance walk?'

'For the time being. Olaf drove me back to the campsite between here and Kenvarloe. Kalendra it's called. So now I'm glad to be of use at *Flotsam Follies*. I might stop on a bit. D'you think that's crazy?'

Not if he wanted to get to know Pippa better, she thought, but didn't say so. 'It's not crazy if that's what you want to do.'

'They've so little business sense between them, you see. I think I can help them get

65

Flotsam Follies off the ground. I'm going to try anyway.'

'A veritable Sir Galahad.'

He smiled. 'You said it, maid. Shall we go?'

She stood up, recovered now, and walked with him along the narrow cobbled streets until they were back at *Flotsam Follies*.

Olaf emerged from his workshop rubbing his hand dry on a ragged towel. 'Pippa had a thought,' he said. 'Any good at water colours, Nicole? Zelda said you'd been to Art College.'

'Not too bad if pushed.'

'We need a background painted for a beach scene.'

'A beach scene?' she said, intrigued.

'A picture of a beach,' Daniel said as if she found it hard to understand. She shot him a reproving look and he grinned back at her. 'I'll need to get some paints,' she said.

Pippa looked pleased 'We've got plenty here somewhere,' she said. 'I'll dig them out for you.'

'So what exactly do you need a beach scene for?'

'As a background to a display of little boats Olaf plans to make. We thought it would make them look really good.'

'It will, definitely,' said Daniel with approval.

Nicole glanced at him and then back at Olaf. 'I'll give it a go, if you like,' she said. 'If it's any good it'll be a thank you for all these lifts you give me. Can I work on it at Kenvarloe?'

Olaf nodded. 'Of course. Take your time with it, Nicole. And thanks.'

Pippa was busy rifling through a box down in the workroom. They heard the sound of small items being emptied out on one of the work tables and Pippa's cry of glee as she replaced them.

'There's plenty in here,' she called up. Pippa brought the box up to show them. 'We picked them up at a car boot sale a week or two back. A bargain. Oh, and there's a pad of watercolour paper somewhere.' She looked round vaguely. 'You'll need brushes. Yes, here they are.'

Daniel took the box from her. 'Where's the van?'

'I'll take it,' said Olaf. 'We're just off. You'll cope here all right till we get back, Daniel?'

Daniel raised his hand in a salute. 'I'll have cleared half the stock by the time you stagger back in. Trust me.'

They left, laughing.

*   *   *

By the time Nicole got in, Zelda was well on with her preparations for the next day even with one arm in plaster. Her face looked flushed as she turned round from taking a batch of the extra-large rolls from the oven

67

and she rubbed her floury hand across her forehead. 'How did you get on in Trevillick, dear?'

Nicole sniffed in appreciation of the gorgeous smell. 'Wonderful. The smell of baking, I mean. *Flotsam Follies* is a dream. I hope they do well. They're off to do a bit of beachcombing now, but they've left someone in charge.'

'And your mobile?'

Nicole had almost forgotten that. 'All present and correct. No new messages.'

'So who have they left in charge at *Flotsam Follies*?'

Nicole frowned. 'Daniel Murray.'

Zelda looked interested. 'Daniel Murray? Wasn't he the nice young chap who escorted you here on Monday when you weren't well and then was so anxious to be off?'

'That's the one. He hurt his shoulder. Olaf drove him to the campsite at Kalendra and he's decided to stay on for a while.'

Zelda was thrilled when she told her about painting the beach scene for them and then wanted to inspect the shell Nicole had bought with her money. 'It's a present from me, dear,' she said. 'I'm glad you found something you like.'

Nicole smiled as she ran her hand across the smooth surface of the shell. 'Thank you, Zelda. I'll treasure it always.' She felt a surge of happiness. Making new friends was great in this delightful place. She wondered, for a fleeting moment, if she could find work in the area and stay on here. But then she thought of Mark's easy assumption that he was part of Zelda's future and it gave her pause.

They lingered over their lunch outside until two young walkers arrived in their thick jerseys and solid hiking boots. Nicole jumped up at once to serve them the salad-filled rolls they wanted and to provide a jug of Zelda's fruit punch.

It was late afternoon by the time they went on their way and then a party of four older people arrived. As Nicole helped serve their cream teas she was pleased to see that Zelda looked happy and relaxed.

By six o'clock several other cream tea clients had been and gone and they were thinking of making a ham salad for their own meal because it was simple and easy.

Afterwards, Zelda settled down with pen and paper to make out her weekly shopping list to be sent to the shop in Trevillick that had agreed to deliver for the next few weeks.

'I must phone for more cream too,' Zelda said. 'The farm at Pollack keeps me supplied and they deliver too, so there's no problem.'

Nicole carried the box of paint out to inspect the tubes of watercolour that Pippa had unearthed for her. She tipped them out on the table and looked at them in dismay. All of them were twisted and caked with rust. One of cadmium yellow had lost its stopper and was totally unusable. Several had practically no paint left inside them and one or two had lost their labels. 'Any good?' asked Zelda bringing out mugs of tea.

'Most of them are useless. The ultramarine's all right and the alizarin, but there's only a tiny bit of yellow ochre.'

'Can you do anything with those?'

'I'll have a go,' Nicole said doubtfully.

Zelda poured tea and then sat down at the table to inspect the muddled tubes.

'It depends what sort of background scene Pippa wants, a busy beach or masses of empty sand,' Nicole said. 'I was stupid not to ask her. Are they home yet, do you know? I'll go and find out what she wants.'

'I haven't heard the van.'

'I'll check. Pippa can't have looked inside the box. I'll have to find an art shop in town and stock up.'

The van was parked at the back of the next door cottage so neatly that it didn't surprise Nicole that they hadn't heard it arrive.

Pippa opened the door, looking flustered.

Nicole looked at her in concern. 'Are you all right, Pippa?'

'Me?' said Pippa blankly.

'I can come back later,' said Nicole. She hadn't seen Pippa like this before. How well did you have to know someone to insist she told her what was upsetting her? She had felt

70

pressured when Daniel seemed to think she was in need of his help. It wouldn't help to force Pippa into that sort of situation now.

She took a few steps back from the doorway. 'I'll see you tomorrow then,' she said.

Pippa rubbed one hand down the side of her skirt and then looked at it as if she didn't know what she was doing.

Nicole hesitated. 'If we can help in any way . . .'

'No, no, please don't worry.'

Thoughtfully, Nicole left. Telling someone not to worry meant that they would do just that, of course.

The tea that Zelda had poured for her was getting cold. Nicole drank it hurriedly. She heard the van's engine start up. 'Something's wrong next door,' she said at last. 'Some sort of problem. Pippa wouldn't say what it was.'

Zelda smiled. 'They've run out of driftwood, most likely, and need to go off beachcombing to stock up again. That's what usually happens.'

She looked unperturbed as she sat there in the evening sunshine drinking her second mug of tea. Zelda knew her young neighbours far better than she did, Nicole thought. They and their father had been living next door for the past six months and in that time Zelda, generous and kind, would have seen to it that the young brother and sister wanted for nothing if she could provide it.

71

But she wasn't entirely convinced that Zelda had got it right this time. She knew that Daniel had looked after the shop for them today so they could go off beachcombing. The lack of beach finds wasn't the problem. The more likely one was an overflowing workshop that Olaf was unable to get into to do anything with it.

Surely Pippa wasn't upset about that?

OLAF REACTS BADLY

Next morning, Nicole gazed down at the painting on the wooden table in front of her. She had made a start on the sky, mixing the blue paint with a great deal of water so that it looked pale rather than a deep hue that wouldn't enhance the subdued scene she had in mind. Hopefully this would provide a fitting background to whatever Pippa and Olaf planned to display.

She picked up a tissue and dabbed away some of the wash to make a few feathery clouds scattered on the pale blue.

So far there had been no sounds from the cottage next door. Pippa and Olaf might not even be there, she thought, because the van wasn't in evidence. Or maybe they had risen early to get started at the gallery as it was Saturday

She mixed some ultramarine and alizarin crimson on the plate she was using as a palette. Before applying it she gazed out to sea and saw that where the horizon had been clear a few minutes ago, was now blurred. A few dark clouds hovered above the higher ground to the west and looked ominous.

She applied the paint on her brush and then dipped a tissue in clean water and wiped it off. Making a mess of her painting wasn't going to make any difference to the weather and there was nothing she could do about it anyway. She applied herself to the task, trying hard not to glance at the cloud still hovering above the horizon.

Zelda already had a large batch of scones cooling on a wire tray with more in the oven by the time Nicole had come downstairs this morning. Then she had started on the rolls, much slower than usual because of her injury, but determined to do all that was needed.

Nicole, her painting finished, left it to dry on the table outside weighted down with a couple of stones and went indoors to offer help.

Zelda smiled as she saw her and wiped some flour off her nose. 'All under control,' she said happily. 'You could check the flowers on the tables in the tearoom if you like, dear. The water might need topping up. We mustn't forget our lunch and cream tea customers and some of them like to sit indoors.'

'Especially if it's raining,' said Nicole, going to do her bidding.

Zelda looked at her anxiously as she returned to the kitchen. 'You don't think there's rain coming?'

'I hope not,' said Nicole.

But as the evening approached the sky became uniformly grey with a slight hint of moisture in the air. She went out into the garden to see how bad it was. There was always a chance that nothing would come of it. This was finger-crossing time, she thought as she returned to the kitchen.

'We must think positively, Zelda,' she said. 'Let's get the barbecue going early and I'll keep our wet weather things handy just in case. And it wouldn't hurt to cover the chairs with those waterproof sheets you've got.'

Zelda's laugh was rather tremulous, but she looked more cheerful by the time the hour approached and no rain had come. Even the slight drizzle had stopped and there was a glimmer of gold out at sea.

'Let me take over,' Nicole said, taking the spatula from her.

Zelda relinquished it with reluctance and then removed the huge apron covering her green frilly blouse and navy skirt. Her eyes were bright in her flushed face and a lock of fair waving hair fell across her forehead.

Nicole gazed fondly at her as Zelda stepped forward to greet the first of the guests.

Soon the tables were all occupied and the sound of talk and laughter rose in the quiet air, only ceasing for a while as everyone tucked in to the mackerel rolls. The salad bowls were passed from table to table.

In her place at the serving table, Nicole shivered a little when she felt the sudden drop in temperature and the coolness of drizzle on her face. Some of the others were feeling it too and were pulling on jackets and jerseys. Someone produced a waterproof groundsheet and amid much laughter several of the girls huddled underneath it.

Zelda looked as if the change in the weather was her fault. 'We'll have to go inside,' she said.

'But we'd like seconds,' said the leader. 'What's a little rain among friends?'

'Come on, everybody,' said Nicole cheerfully. 'Seconds will be served indoors. It'll be a squash, but who cares as long as we're dry? We'll see you don't miss out on the food.'

'I'll stay on duty out here,' said Zelda as Nicole helped her on with her anorak and crammed a man's sou'wester over her aunt's flowing hair. 'How many are going to have some more?'

There was an enthusiastic response.

Inside, they peeled off their outer garments and left them draped over the chairs in the kitchen. Nicole wished she could push the walls of the tearoom out a couple of metres as they all crowded in and found somewhere to sit.

'This is fun,' someone said.

The rain was harder now. Zelda soon appeared in the kitchen, dripping water, with the extra grilled mackerel. As Nicole slid each one into a roll the laughter in the other room was good to hear.

'They're having a great time, Zelda,' she said. 'And you're the star turn.'

Her aunt smiled. 'I aim to please.'

'Get out of that ridiculous hat and your anorak and we'll carry in the dish.'

A cheer greeted them. Who would think that mackerel fillets slipped inside the rolls would have such an impact? But the rolls were homemade and the mackerel fished from local waters. They appreciated that. Nicole marvelled at their good fortune as she washed her hands at the sink.

She grabbed a towel and dried her hands and then did a little dance of triumph before carrying in an extra dish of tomatoes and handing it round. Zelda's face was glowing from the warmth after the chilly wetness of the garden.

When most of the rolls had gone everyone sat back in their chairs, replete. 'Won't you join us?' someone asked.

Zelda smiled across at Nicole. 'Why not?'

Nicole found spare chairs for them. She loved being part of a friendly group with the chance to join in the laughter and talk.

'We must do this again,' a large lady in a purple top exclaimed, as she put down her glass.

'Wouldn't you like something different on the menu next time?' Zelda said in surprise.

Her new friend beamed. 'As long as mackerel are involved,' she said. 'A mackerel club. What d'you think, folks?'

A babble of ideas burst forth from which it seemed that everyone was in agreement and one or two suggested favourite recipes of their own.

'Well now,' said one of the leaders. 'My wife and I are planning the same walk with different groups every Saturday evening. We'd like to make a regular booking, wouldn't we, Elise?'

She nodded. 'Don's got it all planned and we've got bookings for our Saturday walks from the Tourist Office already. Same walk, same menu, different groups.'

'Could you mange that for about fifteen?' asked Don.

'Of course we can,' said Zelda. Bemused, she sipped her fruit punch.

There was plenty to consider here, Nicole thought as she finished hers. Zelda could have a good thing going even if the mackerel rolls soon palled.

'That's attractive,' said the purple lady suddenly. She pushed her chair back, knocking someone's jersey to the floor. She bent to pick it up and looked round for somewhere to put it. 'That picture on the wall . . . who did that?'

Zelda looked to where she was pointing. 'You like it?'

'Where did you get it?'

Zelda looked pleased. 'You like my driftwood picture. A friend makes them for a living.'

'Charming,' Paula murmured. 'Where's his outlet? My grandson would like that. He's nine tomorrow and I haven't got him anything yet. He'd like that. I simply must have one.'

'It won't be exactly the same. They're all different, you see, because no two pieces of driftwood are alike.'

'Unique,' boomed the man on the other side of her. 'Just as we're all unique, Paula. No two of us are alike.'

'That's right,' said a petite lady in shocking pink. She glanced sideways at Paula as if grateful that she'd had a narrow escape.

'But where can I get one?' Paula demanded.

'They sell them locally,' said Zelda. 'Olaf and his sister have a shop in Trevillick, down one of those narrow streets near the harbour.'

'No good,' said Paula firmly. 'We're not going back that way. I must have it now. Can I purchase this one?'

Zelda looked doubtful. 'It was a present.'

Nicole got up. 'I'll do a bit of checking next door, Zelda.'

Moments later she was back, shaking her head slightly at her aunt. Expecting Olaf to be home was a long shot, and even if he had been he wasn't likely to have any samples of his work at the cottage. A pity. It was a shame to turn down a sale on his behalf.

'Olaf wouldn't mind, surely,' she murmured to Zelda as she sat down again. 'We could get another like it.'

'Can I have a closer look?' Paula said. 'Here, Don, you're nearest.'

'May I?' asked Don. He leaned across to lift the picture from the wall.

By this time it was clear to Nicole that Paula was determined to have her way. The price she offered was double that of the similar ones she had seen in *Flotsam Follies* and she was pleased when at last Zelda accepted.

The customers made ready to leave, pulling on wet cagoules amid as much laughter as there had been all evening. Outside the rain still fell, but the group went cheerfully off into the gloaming to meet their minibus in the village.

'Definitely a successful evening,' Nicole said as she poured hot water into the sink and added washing up liquid.

'And they want to make it a weekly event, involving different people all the time,' said Zelda in wonder. Where they'll find them from, I can't imagine. They're not all holidaymakers.'

'All the better,' said Nicole setting to work. 'It might even catch on in a big way and go on throughout the year.'

'Dream on, my love.'

'Where's your fighting spirit?' said Nicole.

Zelda pulled a face as she sniffed her hands. 'I'll get out all my recipe books and see what I can find. Mackerel recipes, there must be plenty.'

'And if there aren't, we'll make up our own,' said Nicole.

*   *   *

They left most of the clearing up till the morning. Both were up early and while they were busy Olaf appeared at the open kitchen door. He hadn't shaved and his long thin face was pale.

'Pippa's upset,' he said.

Zelda looked alarmed. 'What's wrong?'

'We're not going in this morning. We were back late last night.'

'I'd better go in and see her,' said Zelda, wiping her hands dry and thrusting the towel in the laundry basket. 'Give Olaf a cup of tea or something, Nicole. He looks as if he needs it.'

The water in the kettle was already hot and when it boiled Nicole stuffed tea bags in the two largest mugs and picked up the biscuit tin. 'We'll take it in the other room,' she said. 'It's tidier in there.'

He followed her as if in a dream. She knew it was no use questioning him further. He was obviously worried about his sister and she liked him for that.

'No more,' he said when she offered the biscuits again. He leaned back in his chair and glanced round the room. 'It's gone,' he said.

'Oh, the picture,' she said. 'Good news, Olaf. One of last night's customers liked it and insisted on buying it for double its normal price so it's a huge profit for you.'

He sprang upright in his chair, looking appalled. 'You sold it?'

'This person couldn't get to the shop, you see, and she needed it urgently.' Nicole hadn't expected this reaction from him and her voice faltered. 'Zelda knew she could replace it, of course. There was so much admiration for it last night. We thought you'd be pleased.'

He drummed his long thin fingers on the table. 'I make each one with its own character. I can't make another exactly like it.'

She stared at him, bewildered. 'Where's your eye for business, Olaf?'

He scraped his chair back and got up. 'Business, you say. It's art, inspired by the sea and the air and should be fully appreciated.'

'But of course we appreciate it. And so did a lot of people last night. It was good publicity for you.'

He gazed wildly round the room and left.

Nicole, confused, watched him go. She had been too hasty, thinking too much about profit instead of understanding Olaf's feelings about the sale of his gift. How could she have been so insensitive, blundering about thinking she was being clever when in fact she had been nothing more than an interfering fool?

She stared at the empty space on the wall where the picture had been. There was nothing they could do about it now.

Zelda returned as Nicole was carrying the tray into the kitchen. 'Pippa's tired, that's all,' she said. 'She had a sleepless night. I gather Olaf had a bit of a row with their father when they went down to Newlyn to see him yesterday evening.'

'So she won't go in today?'

Zelda looked closely at Nicole. 'Why, what's the matter, dear?'

Nicole hated telling her about Olaf's reaction to the missing painting, but it had to be done.

'Take no notice,' Zelda said airily. 'He'll get over it.'

Nicole hoped she was right. That little scene had been upsetting.

They worked quickly after that, setting the kitchen to rights and when it was done Zelda suggested Nicole take time off. She agreed at once and she set out along the path to the headland with the fresh breeze on her face, loving the feeling of freedom. Blue sea sparkled beyond the eye hole in the highest rock called the Dancing Hole and she climbed right up to it to gaze through. Then she came down and sat with her back against another and looked to the south to Witten Head in the distance and the cliffs beyond that.

Here, with the sunshine on her face and the sound of the surf below, she let her mind wander. She picked a piece of wild thyme from a clump near her and held it to her nose, inhaling the bitter-sweet scent, reminded suddenly of Daniel finding her here when she hadn't expected to see him.

He had walked from Trevillick on his way south on the coast path, but had stopped to help her when she felt weak and dizzy. Now, he was back in town looking after *Flotsam Follies* to enable Olaf and his sister to go off beachcombing when they needed to.

What a life those two had, spending all day on beaches searching for the things they regarded as treasure while Daniel put his plans on hold to help them out. He was probably working at the gallery today. Could it be that Olaf was merely using Daniel? Or maybe he wanted to keep his sister out of Daniel's way? Then she laughed at herself for letting her imagination run away with her.

She looked up and saw Pippa tripping lightly along the path towards her, her loose hair flying in the breeze.

'Nicole,' she called.

Nicole got up. 'Are you all right, Pippa? Olaf was worried about you.'

Pippa smoothed down her long skirt. 'I'm fine.' Her eyes seemed suddenly enormous and her mouth trembled. 'We went down to Newlyn to see Dad last night and were late back.'

Nicole sprang up. 'Sit down, Pippa,' she said. She found a perch nearby and leaned towards her.

Pippa took a gasping breath as she did as she said. 'The gallery means a lot to Olaf, you see.'

Nicole nodded. 'He's so clever making all those things.'

'But we haven't sold many.'

'He told you that one of our customers last night admired the one he gave Zelda and insisted she buy it? Loads of others liked it, too.'

'He didn't tell me that.'

'It was good publicity for *Flotsam Follies*, Pippa,' Nicole said. 'We know you need all you can get and that's why Zelda let it go. She'll replace it, of course. You could make a lot more sales if everyone tells their friends.'

'We hoped people would just see the shop and come in to look around.'

Nicole looked at her in despair. She had a surprising urge to shake some business sense into her. And into Olaf too. What a pair of innocents!

84

Pippa was looking down at her feet now, toeing a loose piece of turf. 'Dad doesn't like Olaf's work,' she said. 'He thinks he's just messing about with bits of wood and that's what they were arguing about. He plans to buy the gallery when our lease runs out.'

'But isn't that good?'

'Dad'll use it as an outlet for his paintings and let Olaf have just a small area for his. It won't seem like our gallery any more, *Flotsam Follies*. He'll change the name of course.'

Nicole was silent for a moment, thinking about it. 'So you need to work extra hard these next few weeks to make *Flotsam Follies* the success it deserves to be,' she said at last. 'That way Olaf will prove to your father that he knows what he's doing.'

Pippa smiled. 'You're good for us, Nicole, believing in what we're doing. And thanks for selling that picture and making your clients interested.'

'We didn't have to try very hard,' said Nicole.

'I saw Zelda,' Pippa said as she got to her feet. 'There's been a phone message for you, but it's not from your sister.'

Bradley? Nicole found it difficult to breathe. All the heat of the day vanished along with the sea surge, the flowers, the breeze, the birdsong.

She ran back to Kenvarloe Cottage.

85

BRADLEY GETS IN TOUCH

Flotsam Follies was well named, Daniel thought, leaning back in the driftwood chair Olaf had made. He looked about him at the displays on the table and shelves, and yawned. Then he got out his mobile and dialled. No signal, obviously, where Olaf was at this moment.

He had sent the pair of them off for the day to meet Adrian, a friend of his in his home town in Dorset who had turned a simple idea into a superb business opportunity. From him they could learn a great deal, he felt sure. The advice would be invaluable to anyone setting up on their own and especially to Olaf and his sister.

Daniel reached out to pick up a small boat with sails of deep purple that enhanced the beauty of the naturally whitened driftwood from which the vessel had been made. He ran his fingers over the hull, examined the tiny stitches in the sail with approval and then put the boat back in position.

With luck Olaf and Pippa would be too engrossed to be bothered with mobile phones and had forgotten they had promised to phone him when they got to Lyme Regis.

Or perhaps by this time they were watching the stone balancing demonstration they had been promised or sunning themselves on the beach making plans to market their own creative work to greater advantage. They might even be sussing out the local bird life. Olaf was a fine birdwatcher and very knowledgeable. Where birds were concerned he sprang to life immediately. Gone was the laid-back chap, dreamily inventing these objects he hoped would catch the eyes of passers-by. But now, hopefully, all that was going to change.

Daniel yawned again, aware that he was doing no good sitting here half asleep when not one potential customer had crossed the threshold since he'd arrived. He ought to shut up shop and have done with it but if he did that Olaf would appear and demand to know what he thought he was doing when he'd offered his services this fine day.

He leaned back a little too far, lost his balance and slid onto the floor. He lay for a moment gazing up at the rafters, admiring the pattern they made against the steep roof.

There was plenty of space to spare up there to put in another floor, he thought. It was a pity Olaf and his sister only rented the place. He could put them in touch with an architect pal of his who could do a good job on this and would know a good reasonably priced local builder who would make a fine job of it. With the extra space they could have another showroom, serve coffee. But that was going too far. He couldn't imagine Olaf agreeing to anything like that.

Daniel leapt to his feet in one easy movement and righted the chair. If it hadn't been well made he might have smashed it with his antics. Olaf was a clever chap with wood. He had imagination as well as expertise and the gift of making others see what he saw. If there was anything he could do to further his success, then so be it.

Olaf and his sister needed help and because of his injured shoulder he was able to give it. Even better, the remorse he carried around with him was pushed to the back of his mind for a while when he was here doing his bit and that was good too.

He'd give it another half hour and then get back to his campsite at Kalendra, have a shower and then go for a pizza at the camp café before heading off for Kenvarloe to hear how Pippa and Olaf had got on today.

*　　*　　*

The sudden sea mist hovered about the headlands to the south and then came rolling north so that in no time it seemed to Nicole that the headland rocks were dark shapes in the swirling white. It was colder now, too, and Nicole huddled further into the gap between two of the highest, glad that for a time at least she was invisible.

'I tried to get the number but it was withheld,' Zelda had said as soon as Nicole burst into the kitchen after talking to Pippa. A frown had wrinkled her forehead and she held her plastered arm across her chest.

Nicole hated to see her so worried. 'It was Bradley, wasn't it? What did he say?'

'He said he'd be in touch.'

'But how did he know I was here?'

'Harriet?'

'Harriet wouldn't tell anyone.'

'Now don't panic, dear,' said Zelda, looking as if she was about to do that herself.

Nicole took a deep breath and then struggled to sound uncaring. 'Bradley's a bit of a nuisance, that's all, Zelda. Don't worry about it. I can deal with him.'

'If he shows up here he'll have me to deal with.' Her aunt sounded so fierce that Nicole giggled.

'By waving your spatula at him?' she said. 'Alerting all your customers to form an ambush, hitting him with your plastered arm?'

'Should we tell Mark about it?' said Zelda, brightening a little.

'Why not?' If it made Zelda feel better, Nicole thought, then what was the harm? She would think of Bradley no more.

But all the next day she found herself dwelling on him too much for her own good. When the tea things had been cleared she reached for her jacket on the peg near the

89

door.

'You're not going out?' Zelda said in surprise. 'It's still misty out there. You'll be careful, dear, and not go too near the edge? It's getting thicker by the minute.'

'I'm only going to the headland,' Nicole said. 'I'll be safe there, I promise. I need space to think, to work something out.'

But there was nothing to work out, Nicole thought, huddling in her hiding place with her hands round her knees. She couldn't move on somewhere else and leave Zelda to cope on her own with the tearoom after she had promised her help.

She had to play a waiting game, hoping that in time Bradley would find someone else to appreciate him and would leave her alone. She had made her feelings clear enough from the beginning. Unfortunately he was unable to accept it.

She raised her face. Around her the mist swirled, sometimes thick and sometimes thinning a little so that she could see a short way along the cliff path. When she saw Daniel striding along she knew instantly who he was and her heart quickened.

She must have made some movement because he looked up towards her.

'Hi there, Nicole. Playing hide and seek?'

'I wish,' she said. 'I'm a coward, that's all. I was almost thinking of running away from Kenvarloe.'

'I don't believe that.'

His raised face was so full of surprise tinged with anxiety that she was suddenly overcome.

He scrambled up to her. 'Nicole, what's wrong?'

His breath was warm on her face as he leaned near and put a comforting arm round her shoulders. She leaned against him, feeling the beating of his heart, glad he was here at this moment. After a while she rubbed her eyes and pulled away, ashamed that she had nearly given way to tears.

Concern shone from his eyes. 'Can't you tell me what's worrying you?' he said. He moved away slightly so he could see her face.

'I . . . I . . .' she began and then paused to reach for a tissue and scrubbed at her eyes.

It was a relief to tell him about Bradley and how she had hoped he had got the message to leave her alone and then found that he hadn't. The good intentions she had made to forget about him because he was miles away had foundered because of the phone call yesterday evening.

Daniel said nothing for a moment, but reached out to pick a piece of thyme and hold it to his nose. 'These flowers never change,' he said. 'Year in, year out we'll discover them finding difficult footholds in this rocky place. They never give up. And neither must you, Nicole. You know that. You've made a brilliant start coming here; getting on with your life. You've done the best you can to put it behind you.'

'The phone call to the cottage . . .'

'Even if someone told him your aunt's number he won't know the address, will he?'

She thought for a moment, staring across at the invisible cottage in the distance. 'No-one knows I'm here, only my sister and she's a soul of discretion. It frightens me not knowing how he knows.'

Daniel looked thoughtfully at the small mauve flower in his hand. 'Leavey's an unusual name and it's your aunt's as well as yours. He could have looked it up in the phone book.'

'But how would he know which one to choose?'

'A blind shot?' Daniel said. 'Working his way through all of them?'

In that case her whereabouts would definitely be known. She saw that the thought had hit Daniel at the same time.

'But if he turns up here, so what?' he said, looking troubled.

She hesitated. 'Well, yes, I see what you mean. What can he do really except be a nuisance?'

'He can't stay around here forever,' Daniel pointed out. 'I can't see your aunt welcoming him with open arms, forcing barbecued mackerel on him and insisting he move in at once?'

Nicole smiled, feeling better now. 'Zelda

already has plans for attacking him if he shows up. And she made me agree to her telling Mark to look out for him in Trevillick. Although I don't know what Mark would do if he did. It's hardly a crime for strangers to be around. You would be clapped into gaol if it was, wouldn't you?'

Instead of smiling as she expected Daniel snapped off a stalk of grass and put the end in his mouth. 'Concentrate on those mackerel suppers, why don't you?' he said, his voice serious. 'Physical action is a big help, Nicole, all that barbecuing of mackerel and serving the needs of others.' He grinned. 'I'm sure you're up for it.'

She nodded. 'I'm sure you're right.'

'I find physical activity helps.' He looked away from her, one shoulder hunched.

'You've got a problem too?' She was surprised.

'I wasn't always this confident know-all you see before you who strides the coast paths of England.' He kicked at a loose pebble and watched it tumble down a grassy patch and come to rest against a bigger stone. 'I did something disgraceful once on holiday in Crete when I wanted to impress some other lads I met there. We set off in pedaloes to circumnavigate the island of Spinalonga. Foolhardy, I know. The others turned back, but not me. Oh no, I knew it all. Sheer bravado.'

'What happened?'

'It was like shooting the rapids when I was round the other side. The current was terrifying. I was being swept out to sea and I panicked. Someone raised the alarm and a couple of chaps came out to me. One of them got into difficulties himself. He could have drowned. Then the lifeguards got there, risking their own lives because of me being stupid. I wanted to buy them a meal or something when we got back to shore, but they'd have none of it.'

There was silence for a long moment. Then he said, 'I didn't know where to put myself I was so ashamed.'

'And in deep shock too, I should think,' Nicole said, her voice gruff with sympathy.

'I suppose I was,' he said. He turned towards her and she saw that there were shadows under his eyes. 'I have nightmares sometimes about what could have happened.'

She was shaken by a sudden longing to put her arms round him and offer comfort as he had done for her a moment ago.

'So then what did you do?'

He shrugged. 'I haven't told anyone this before.'

She felt absurdly pleased, but deeply sorry for him at the same time as she pictured that poor terrified young boy.

'And you've carried that around with you ever since?' she said.

'Daft isn't it?'

Not if you're deeply sensitive, she wanted to say, but thought better of it. What he had told her was deeply moving but she felt unable to express this without sounding patronising. He was a good man, genuinely concerned about others.

'I threw myself into every physical activity I could think of to try to forget,' he said. 'I even got a job at an outdoor leisure centre place in Wales after I left school. Then I got myself qualified as a sailing instructor, moved back to Dorset and worked for a while in the family restaurant. Ideal for giving sailing instruction in my spare time.

'Now I'm an accountant. A big jump I know.' He grinned at her. 'I'm full of surprises. But somehow I found myself at university and then did my accountancy exams. Now I work in a firm in Lyme Regis, my home town. I'm fairly content, but sometimes this other thing rears up and I need to be on the move. I save up my leave and take off, doing something to tire me physically.'

'This time walking part of the south west coastal path?'

'It helps, you see. There's something about wild, remote areas that I find satisfying,' he said. 'It's not just the physical thing, tiredness and all that. There's something else, some spiritual feeling of wellbeing I can't explain. It's natural, not built by man. It's been here

95

hundreds, thousands of years. Millions even.'

'It's quite a thought,' she said.

He nodded. 'But then I injured my shoulder and was stuck here for a while. Luckily for me I found someone who needed some help and decided to do what I could.'

'*Flotsam Follies*?' she said.

'Does it sound ridiculously pious and smug?'

She shook her head. 'Not if it helps. And your shoulder?'

He wriggled it, smiling. 'As good as new.'

'So you'll be moving on?'

'Not for a while. Not while there's a job here to be done.'

She said nothing for a moment while she thought about it. 'Zelda's fond of Olaf and Pippa and wants to help them,' she said at last. 'But it's not easy.' She hesitated again for a moment and told him about Olaf's fury about the sale of his picture.

'Olaf's in a world of his own,' Daniel said. 'I sent them off to see a friend of mine today who can demonstrate how to get a business like theirs off the ground. I'm hoping it'll inspire them.'

On their first meeting she had misjudged him because he reminded her of Bradley and that was totally unfair. His kindness to her and to others was part of his nature but she was aware, suddenly, that his friendship was something to be valued.

She got to her feet.

Daniel got up too, looked once more at the twig of thyme and then put it in the pocket of his shorts. The cottages were in view now, but looked dim in the poor visibility.

'I came to find out how Olaf got on,' he said. His voice softened. 'And Pippa too of course. Have they got back yet?'

She considered. 'Oh yes, I saw Pippa.'

'Then let's go,' he said, obviously so anxious for action that Nicole felt rebuffed.

He fell into step beside her and then walked behind as the path narrowed. She hastened her pace a little, uncomfortable still with anyone walking directly behind her because of his likeness to Bradley even though she knew this was unreasonable.

'I'm not bothering you, am I?' he said.

She slowed down again. 'Not when I know it's you,' she said.

As they got close to the cottages the ringing tone of Zelda's telephone rang out. Nicole stopped short. Oh no, not again, she thought in dismay. She turned an anguished face to Daniel.

'This could be someone else,' he said. 'Don't overreact.' Ignoring the neighbouring cottage, he caught hold of Nicole's arm and propelled her towards Zelda's. They reached the open door as Zelda replaced the telephone on its hook.

'That was Mark,' she said. 'He's not gone out fishing today because of the weather. He thought he'd better warn me not to expect any more mackerel for the time being. It's going to get worse, he says.'

'I'd better be quick next door and get back to Kalendra while I can,' said Daniel. 'See you then, Nicole. And Zelda.'

Zelda looked enquiringly at her niece. 'Is everything all right, dear?'

'I met Daniel up there on the headland,' Nicole said. She glanced at the telephone on the wall near the fridge. Then she turned her back on it. Let it ring all it liked, she thought, holding herself ready in case it did and she needed to make a bolt for it. Then, relaxing, she smiled.

'Let's make something nice for our evening meal,' said Zelda.

'As long as it's not mackerel,' said Nicole.

Zelda laughed and agreed. Between them they cooked lamb chops to go with new potatoes and salad. They ate at the kitchen table so that clearing away would be easy. Afterwards they made do with biscuits and cheese and an apple apiece which they carried into the sitting room.

Zelda went to the window and peered out at a world that seemed even whiter now than before.

'I hope Daniel gets back to Kalendra all right,' Nicole said.

'That lad's got more sense than to take silly risks,' said Zelda with confidence.

Certainly not now and perhaps never again, Nicole thought.

Zelda left the window and sat down. 'He'll spend the night there, I shouldn't wonder. I can't see Pippa letting him do anything else.'

Nicole was silent, an ache in her heart as she imagined the two of them together. Olaf would be there, too, of course. She must remember that. They would be safe from harm, the three of them, enjoying each other's company, cooking a meal together, laughing.

She looked at Zelda who with her left arm in its plaster resting on the table was managing to cut a piece of cheese with her right hand. She felt a sudden rush of affection for her, coping so well with all life threw at her and making her so welcome when she turned up unannounced. She had made it plain that her home was her place too for as long as she wanted. Here she was surrounded by the love of someone who had her interests at heart.

How could she have even considered leaving because of her fear of Bradley when Zelda needed her? Not only that, but she wouldn't see Daniel again if she moved away and he was beginning to mean a great deal to her.

NICOLE'S FEELINGS FOR DANIEL GROW

Visibility was still poor next morning and hadn't cleared by the time they heard Olaf's van start up with its customary roar at half-past nine.

'No customers for us again today in weather like this,' said Zelda. 'I hope Olaf does better.'

'I hope so,' said Nicole. 'With luck they'll all crowd into the gallery to shelter and he'll do a roaring trade.'

'You're so practical, dear.'

Nicole smiled. 'Someone has to be.'

'You're not suggesting I'm not practical?'

Nicole laughed though she didn't feel much like it. Daniel would have travelled in to Trevillick in the van with Olaf and Pippa for sure. She wondered what his plans were for the day unless he was going to hang round the gallery to keep Pippa company.

She tried not to think of that as she helped Zelda wipe the kitchen surfaces ready for some baking of scones in case someone was foolhardy enough to venture out for a cream tea today.

Zelda hummed to herself as she got the flour out of the cupboard. She had dressed this morning in bright orange cut-offs and a sleeveless blue shirt. 'Are you expecting a visit from Mark?' Nicole asked.

'If he comes he'll tell us when he plans on going out fishing again,' Zelda said.

Nicole glanced towards the window. 'Don't hold your hopes up too high.'

'I know dear. We did so well on Saturday, didn't we? And there's the money to bank.'

'I'll go in by bus and do that if you like, Zelda, and put in an order at the fish shop too.'

'Would you, dear?'

'I can take my beach painting with me and then if Pippa doesn't like it I can do another when I get back. How about me getting another picture from Olaf to replace the one you sold?'

Zelda's dimple deepened as she shot an amused look at her. 'I did well, didn't I? Get a move on then, dear, or you'll miss the bus.'

Nicole changed into a summer skirt and pulled on a light jacket over her T-shirt. Her bag felt pleasantly heavy when Zelda had loaded it with the money taken at the barbecue and she carried her painting rolled up and neatly secured with a rubber band.

As she shut the door behind her, Pippa came running lightly down her front path and waved to her.

'Off to town, Nicole?' she called. 'Could you call in at the shop and tell Olaf we won't be in today? D'you think we could order some lunch from Zelda? Daniel's idea. He'll pay.'

'Better ask her,' Nicole called back.

She hurried up the track. In her effort to keep her voice light she forgot the painting in her hand. Her heart was heavy and she was thankful she was heading for the bus to take her into Trevillick so that she wouldn't have to see Daniel and Pippa at close quarters so plainly absorbed in each other.

*   *   *

She called in at *Flotsam Follies* when the business at the bank and fishmongers was done. For once the gallery was crowded. Olaf looked harassed and was doing his best to cope with prospective customers. Every now and again he glanced towards the door of his workshop.

'Could you use some help?' she asked him in a quiet moment.

His long thin face lit up with a smile. 'Would you, Nicole? I could use some help here in the gallery.'

She nodded and then gave him the message from Pippa, surprised that Olaf showed little concern that she and Daniel wouldn't be in today. He turned to answer a question from a young girl in trim shorts and then looked back at Nicole. 'Thank you. I'm grateful.'

'I'm in no hurry to get back, Olaf,' she said. 'But I'll just phone Zelda to say where I am.'

She looked round for somewhere to put

her painting where Pippa would be sure to see it when she came in tomorrow. Then she got her phone out of her bag, knowing that Zelda would be delighted Olaf was doing so well today.

She settled happily to answer the questions fired at her and to selling a few things. One or two questions had to be passed on to Olaf. He emerged from his workshop, wiping his hands and pleased to talk about his work now that he had the chance of getting on with it.

The time passed happily, but Nicole was aware that only the cheaper objects were selling and when the takings were added up it wasn't a huge amount. Multiply that by seven and it couldn't possibly be enough to pay the rent. She wondered that Olaf didn't seem aware of this, but praised her for the amount she had sold by the end of the afternoon.

She had chosen another driftwood boat picture on a pale background for Zelda, as similar as she could get to the one Olaf had given her. He made no comment when he took the money with the extra that Paula had insisted on paying. She longed to suggest he supply a few more to display for sale in Zelda's tearoom but didn't dare.

Olaf pulled the bolt across the door and then paused and pulled it back again. Mark slipped inside and greeted Nicole with a smile.

'I've come to give you a lift home if this chap can't drag himself away from his work,' he said. 'I'm off to meet one of my suppliers and Kenvarloe's on my way. The car's just round the corner.'

Olaf nodded. 'Thanks for your help, Nicole. Tell that sister of mine I'll stay on here for a while. She'll have plenty to occupy her this evening.'

Nicole left with Mark, her spirits soaring. So Pippa had plenty to occupy her in entertaining Daniel this evening when she had been in his company all day? It was hard not to feel envious at the thought of them together.

Mark said nothing until they reached his car. She looked at him and noticed that the lines round his mouth had deepened. She saw how tired he was by the way his head drooped a little as he got into the driver's seat.

They set off up through the narrow streets.

'The fact is, I can't take time off this week to go out in the boat,' he said. 'I don't like to let Zelda down.'

'She'll understand,' said Nicole.

He nodded. 'Oh yes, she'll understand. But having to collect the fish from town's not so good for her now she's got this mackerel thing going. I don't want Zelda's understanding. I want her happiness.'

She was silent for a moment, aware of the feeling beneath his words.

'There are fillets in the freezer,' she said at last. 'Plenty for Saturday and I'm here to help. I'll come into town on the bus for more. No problem.'

'This is a big thing she's taken on with a broken wrist,' he said. 'She hasn't done evening meals before, only lunches and cream teas. I don't know that I like it.'

He sounded so down that Nicole hesitated. His words sounded as if he and Zelda were deeply involved, but her aunt had given no indication that her arrival had interrupted anything. But of course Zelda wouldn't have wanted to make her feel uncomfortable.

They drove up out of the town. Nicole looked back at the clustered houses and the busy harbour. Out at sea the clouds were clearing. It would be a beautiful evening. She sighed.

'Sorry,' Mark said. They reached the main road and he glanced at her, smiling now though his eyes looked sad. 'Staff problems, that's all. But I shouldn't bother you when you've got worries of your own. Believe me when I say I'll look out for you, Nicole.'

'Thank you, Mark. It's good to have friends.'

'We all need friends.'

'And don't forget I'm here to help Zelda,' she said.

'You're a good girl.'

Nicole smiled at his kind tone. 'I'll see she's all right and can cope with the meals in the evening.'

Mark dropped her at the top of the track down to the cottages. He had no time to lose if he wanted to be in time for his appointment. She watched him go, concerned that he was so anxious.

*   *   *

Later, the washing up done, the two of them sat outside, listening for the sound of arrivals. They couldn't see Pippa and Olaf's cottage from here and Nicole was glad of that because it was painful to be reminded of the time Daniel and Pippa had spent together while she was busy helping out at *Flotsam Follies*. But she had no right to judge, she reminded herself. They were free agents. She was just being pathetic.

Zelda, content with the day's takings for lunch, gazed across at the Dancing Hole on the summit of the rocks on the headland that were sharp against the sea now that the mist had cleared.

'A lovely evening,' she murmured, her expression dreamy.

'I forgot something,' said Nicole. She jumped up to fetch the picture from Olaf's shop she had brought home with her.

With an exclamation of pleasure, Zelda unwrapped the paper bag with her good hand and lifted it out.

Before she had time to say anything they heard footsteps and Olaf appeared round the side of the cottage. He looked odd, a lock of his long hair falling across his forehead.

'I found this,' he said. He held out Nicole's mobile phone.

She took it from him. 'Thanks, Olaf. I didn't realise I'd left it behind.'

He eyed her warily.

Zelda seemed suddenly aware that something was wrong. 'Sit down Olaf,' she said. 'Have you something to tell us?'

He cleared his throat and Nicole knew what was coming.

'So it rang after I'd gone?' she said.

He looked awkward. 'I thought it was you, you see, checking to see where you'd left it.'

'You answered it?'

'I'm sorry. It has nothing to do with me but . . .'

'Don't worry about it, Olaf,' said Nicole with as much firmness as she could manage. 'I don't know what he said but it's my problem. It's under control.' She couldn't help her voice trembling a little as she finished speaking.

Zelda leaned towards Olaf and took his hand. 'It's good of you to be concerned for Nicole, dear, but there's really no need.'

Olaf nodded but he still looked unhappy. He got to his feet.

'I love my new picture,' said Zelda. She picked it up and held it close to her. 'And I promise you, Olaf, I won't sell it on this time. It will be safe on my bedroom wall for evermore.'

He smiled. 'I'm glad to hear that, Zelda.'

'But now there's a gap on the wall in the tearoom. Won't you be a dear and let me display more of your work there? Another outlet for it must be a good idea surely?'

He looked unconvinced. 'We need all I make for the gallery. I didn't get on too well after you left, Nicole. It was worrying, that phone call, whatever you say. I wasn't sure what I should do.'

'You did the right thing in bringing the phone here,' said Zelda firmly.'

He nodded, and left.

Nicole shifted a little on her seat, aware that his work had suffered because of her carelessness in leaving her mobile behind. She hadn't asked what Bradley had said, but Olaf must have cut him off or he would have passed on a message surely? Or maybe Bradley had been offensive on hearing a man's voice? Whatever it was, she was distressed that Olaf had had to deal with it.

She seemed to cause trouble wherever she went.

SPENDING TIME WITH DANIEL

Nicole spent a restless night. She got up once or twice to open her bedroom curtains to peer out at the shimmering sea, glad that the sky was still clear and the mist had gone. The moonlight trickled over the intervening rough ground, casting small shadows.

She awoke late. Seeing the time, she sprang out of bed. The sun was well up, shining into the corners of the room.

'I thought we'd eat outside this glorious morning,' Zelda greeted her.

Nicole eyed the tray loaded with fruit juice and glasses. The smell of grilled bacon and freshly brewed coffee filled the kitchen. 'You're spoiling me,' she said.

'You'll have to do the carrying,' said Zelda. 'I've already wiped the tables and chairs and taken out some cushions.'

'You think of everything.'

Zelda's dimple deepened as she smiled. 'Did you hear the phone?'

Nicole was instantly alert. 'The phone?'

'I've invited a guest to breakfast. He'll be here soon. He had to collect a hired car from Trevillick.'

Nicole glanced at the tray and saw that there were three glasses on it. 'Mark?' she said.

'Daniel. He phoned on the off-chance and I invited him to join us for breakfast. I took his mobile number and put it in the book in case he gets held up.'

'The off-chance of what, a free meal?'

'Don't be silly, dear. He wanted Pippa to go out with him for the day, but apparently Olaf can't do without her.'

'I see.' Nicole picked up the tray and carried it out into the freshness of the morning. She unloaded and took the tray back inside, leaving the door wide open. 'So where was Daniel planning to take Pippa?' she asked.

Zelda looked at her anxiously. 'It was something he booked without telling her,' she said. 'He can't pull out of the arrangement now so he suggested he take you instead.'

Nicole was suspicious. 'Take me where?'

'He said you'd see why when you get there.'

'So I'm just a stand-in?'

'Don't be like that, dear. He means well.'

'But what about you, Zelda? You'll have people pouring in for refreshments today in lovely weather like this. You need me here.'

'Mark will come if I get too busy.'

'And neglect all those problems at his market garden?'

'He told you about that?'

'There's some sort of conspiracy going on here and I'm not sure I like it.'

Zelda looked apologetic. 'I have your interest at heart, dear, that's all. It'll do you good to get away somewhere, Nicole dear, and relax for a while.'

Nicole let out the breath she had been holding, ashamed of her ungracious reaction, but no-one with any self-respect liked playing second best. And how could she relax in. Daniel's company knowing she must hide her

110

growing feelings for him?

'Anyway, you'll hear all about it any minute now,' Zelda said. 'Here he is.'

Nicole listened to the sound of an approaching vehicle with misgivings.

The white Citroen pulled up and Daniel got out.

'Hi there,' he called. 'What d'you think? Luxury or what?'

He seemed different today in his faded blue sweatshirt and jeans, Nicole thought. He looked so cheerful that no-one would guess he'd been disappointed in his first choice of companion for a day out. But his tact would have seen to that. She had to hand it to him. Well, she could play a part, too.

She smiled a welcome. 'Hi there, Daniel.'

'So your aunt's filled you in?' he looked at her expectantly, his head a little to one side. 'Are you game to come with me? You won't regret it.'

'Bring the coffee pot, will you, Nicole?' Zelda said. 'And Daniel, the bacon's to go inside these rolls. Could you see to that?'

He sprang to obey.

Outside, the table was in full sunshine and for a while there was silence as they sipped their orange juice and Zelda handed round the rolls.

'This is perfect,' said Daniel at last. 'Can I lick my fingers?' He did just that without waiting for permission and then leaned back

111

in his seat as Zelda poured coffee. 'We won't linger, Nicole, great as this is. Lyme Regis calls.'

Nicole was surprised. 'Lyme Regis?'

'This is a special arrangement today since Olaf and Pippa let me down so badly. They got sidetracked on their way to see my friend, would you believe, gave up and came home.'

'Bird watching?' asked Nicole with interest.

'Keen as I am on birds, I was none too pleased since I'd offered to look after the shop for them. I almost sold something, too.'

He sounded so aggrieved that Zelda laughed. 'Sounds typical of those two.'

'Not another Great Northern Diver?' said Nicole.

'A pair of choughs spotted on the cliffs at Portangle. Olaf picked it up on the van radio. Much more important to him than learning something to his advantage if he carried on to Lyme.'

Perplexed, Nicole looked from one to the other.

Daniel drained his coffee cup and smiled at her. 'You don't know what I'm talking about, Nicole, do you?'

Intrigued in spite of herself, she shook her head. This was beginning to sound more promising. Olaf and Pippa had let Daniel down. He had been disappointed and annoyed too, by the sound of it.

Daniel got up. 'We'd better be off. It's a

long way.'

Nicole collected her bag and jacket and was ready. Zelda gave her a hug. 'Enjoy yourself, dear. And don't worry about anything.'

Daniel was a careful driver, perhaps not used to the hired car, Nicole thought. Slowly he drove up the track, paused to check no-one was coming and then set off at a faster speed through Kenvarloe and out onto the main road.

'You haven't told me much about Lyme Regis,' she said.

'It's a pretty town by the sea in Dorset, on the side of a hill, with a harbour. You must have heard of the Cobb that's part of the harbour wall and that it's on the Jurassic Coast?'

'Dinosaurs? That sort of thing?'

'You got it in one. You don't see many of those about these days.'

'Shame.'

'Fossils, though.'

'All that,' she agreed. 'And?'

He laughed, obviously enjoying teasing her. 'Wait and see.'

She had to wait longer than he anticipated because there was a hold-up near Exeter that delayed them for twenty minutes. But once on the A35 they made good time and drove slowly down the town's steep main street with enticing views of sparkling sea and distant headlands beyond.

113

'We've just time to park and grab a portable coffee on the way down to the beach,' Daniel said.

He drove up a narrow side street, turned into a cobbled yard and parked the car by the far wall. They got out and stretched and then he vanished through a door in the adjoining building to emerge minutes later with two lidded polystyrene cups of coffee.

The breeze ruffled Nicole's hair as they walked down the busy street and along the sea front. Daniel came to a sudden stop. 'He's here. Look!'

Nicole looked and saw a group of people leaning on the railings gazing at the beach. The man they had obviously come to see had arranged a large hoop of wood on the pebbly sand. In this he had planted two huge smooth boulders standing on end. Nearby was a stand of cards, another of what looked like mounted prints and a table and chair.

The man turned round, spotted Daniel and waved.

'Hi, Adrian,' Daniel called, raising his hand in salute.

They'd driven a long way for this, Nicole thought. The sparkling sea met the shore in a ripple of splashing foam. Squawking seagulls wheeled and swooped in the salty air. As at Trevillick, people lingered at the waterside gazing at the boats in the harbour or across the beach to the sea beyond. She had a quick look round at the spectators, checking as she always did for a familiar face. Strangers, all of them. She gazed back at the beach.

Adrian picked up a smaller oval-shaped boulder, also smooth. Concentrating hard, he lifted it to rest delicately on the rounded top of the first one. A gasp came from the audience who seemed to have been holding their collective breath.

The surface wasn't even flat, Nicole saw. It was impossible for it to stay there. Awed, she was silent for a long moment. 'I don't believe I saw him do that,' she said at last.

'Clever, wouldn't you say?' said Daniel.

She nodded and stared, expecting the top boulder to crash down on the sand at any minute. But it was still balanced there, proudly aloft, looking as if there was some sort of glue holding it in place.

Daniel removed the lid on his cup and drank. 'I needed that.'

Still bemused, Nicole did the same. Daniel took the empty containers and looked round for a litter bin. By the time he came back Adrian had picked up another boulder and it, too, was balanced on its base. This time it was slightly to one side of the more pointed top. How it stayed there she couldn't imagine. It was magic. She could feel it in the air about her. And so could others by their bemused expressions.

One or two people jumped down on the

beach to examine and buy the cards. Adrian moved among them, distinguishable by the brown-brimmed hat he wore. Then he seated himself at the table to take their money and answer questions.

Nicole was still gazing at his handiwork, expecting any minute that something mysterious would happen because the laws of nature had gone awry.

'Nature's glue, he calls it.' Daniel's voice in her ear broke her trance. 'Brilliant, isn't it? People seem to like it.'

She could see that from the number of cards being sold. Someone was interested in a large signed print of a close-up of a spectacular balance of a split boulder that leant gracefully to one side of a bigger one beneath. Adrian got up from his seat and held the print up for the man to see more clearly.

'It's one of the hardest balances I've done,' he said. 'It was almost impossible to find the centre. It collapsed over twenty times before I found the sweet spot. You can see the scrape marks on the bottom boulder.'

The man peered at it, nodded and pulled out his wallet.

People were moving away now and when most of them had gone Daniel jumped down on the beach too and held out a hand to support Nicole as she joined him.

'Adrian,' he said. 'I've brought Nicole to see your work.'

'I wasn't expecting anything like this,' she said. 'It's a miracle.'

He smiled. 'Gravity, that's all.'

'He's being modest,' Daniel said. 'He's been creating these compositions of wonder for years, ever since I've known him. He does demonstrations all over the place now. His work features in offices, hotels and other places too. His website reaches millions . . .'

'You don't know that,' said Adrian.

'If it doesn't it should do. It's the perfect way to do business.'

Nicole smiled at Daniel's enthusiasm. 'Does anyone else do this sort of thing?' she asked.

'His work's unique,' said Daniel as if that ended the matter.

A young father in a sleeveless shirt, clutching his young son by the hand, was gazing in wonder too.

Adrian obviously had an imagination and vision not everyone had, Nicole thought. Like Olaf's ability to see the shapes of things in the driftwood he found. Daniel's friend had fostered a weird kind of imagination in himself and built this through persistence and determination into a successful business. He wouldn't have a website that impressed Daniel if he hadn't done that. And how fortunate he was to be able to earn his living doing something that obviously meant so much to him. Not many people could do that.

She glanced at Daniel, still deep in

conversation but also including others too. He picked up some of the cards to show them.

She smiled and felt for her purse to buy some too.

More spectators were leaning on the railings now, intrigued. Adrian removed the top boulders he had balanced so cleverly earlier and then replaced them amid more gasps of admiration.

'Seen enough now, Nicole?' said Daniel.

'I'll never see enough,' she said in humility. She felt in her pocket for her shell and smoothed it between finger and thumb. In some odd way the sensation made her feel suddenly happy. There was magic in the air around her and she knew it had a lot to do with being here with Daniel. She didn't want this moment to end.

They said their farewells and walked back along the busy sea front and up the steep street the way they had come. Daniel ignored the turning into the narrower one to reach the car. Instead he opened the door of a small restaurant and ushered her inside.

'My parents' place,' he said.

AN AWKWARD MEETING

Nicole stood on the threshold and gazed at the long low room. She felt as if she had been transported to the bottom of the sea. The bright matting beneath her feet seemed like golden sand. Glass fish swam on turquoise walls, highlighted from within by a myriad of sparkling colours. '

'Amazing isn't it?' said Daniel's voice in her ear.

She took a deep breath as she move d inside. The tables painted green and the chairs of roughened white wood made her think of Olaf miles away in Trevillick.

Daniel caught hold of her arm and propelled her towards a seat in the window. They were the only customers.

Bemused, she seated herself. He picked up the menu written on paper in the shape of a fish. 'Hungry?'

She hadn't been until now. She smiled. 'You're full of surprises.' He looked pleased. 'You like it here?'

'Daniel!' A tall, slim woman in navy trousers and white linen top came forward eagerly to greet him.

Daniel leapt to his feet and gave her a hug. 'Mum, surprise, surprise!'

His mother, smiling, broke away and turned to Nicole. Her perfume was light and flowery and seemed to be born on the movement of air that stirred the hangings at the open window. 'I'm so glad you are here with Daniel, my dear. We've heard so much about you.'

'You have?' said Nicole in surprise.

'I've brought Nicole to meet you, Mum,' said Daniel as he sat down again.

His mother looked taken aback. 'Nicole?

The temperature in the room seemed suddenly to drop.

'Hello, Nicole. No, don't get up, dear. How nice to meet you.'

Feeling awkward, Nicole subsided in her chair with the feeling she shouldn't really be here. 'And you, too, Mrs Murray,' she said.

'Daniel's father, James, has popped out for a while. He'll be back soon. I'm Felicity.'

'So who's doing the cooking?' asked Daniel.

His mother smiled. 'We've got someone new all the way from Sussex. He's good. I think he finds it a bit too quiet here, but I hope he'll stay.'

'At least long enough to cook our meal,' said Daniel.

Felicity looked at him fondly and Nicole had the impression she would like to have ruffled his hair.

'Sit down, Mum, and join us why don't you?'

'I'm on duty behind the scenes, dear. Maybe later, for coffee, or will you come upstairs for a while?'

'We've a long journey ahead of us,' said Daniel.

At that moment the door from the street burst open. The man who came in looked so much like Daniel with his shock of fair hair and friendly smile that he could be no other than Daniel's father, Nicole thought as she rose to be introduced.

Her hand was gripped tightly. 'So your brother's not with you today?' he said. 'That's a shame. I'd like to have met him. He sounds an interesting chap from what Daniel here says. Busy, is he?'

'As far as I know Nicole hasn't got a brother, Dad,' said Daniel. 'And if she had he wouldn't be Olaf.'

His father looked confused. 'You mean ...?'

'That's right, Dad. This is Nicole not Pippa.'

His mother moved back a pace, shot a look of embarrassment at Nicole and then hastily withdrew. 'I'll see you both later,' she called back over her shoulder. An inner door banged shut behind her.

They sat down again. James Murray, looking ill at ease, stood with one hand on the back of a chair. He cleared his throat. 'Have I put my foot in it?'

'Don't worry about it, Dad. We don't.'

Nicole smiled at him. Daniel sounded as if he really meant it, but all the same a small feeling of uneasiness gripped her because of the awkwardness in the atmosphere. 'I think Daniel hoped to inspire Olaf and Pippa to better business practices by showing them his friend at work on the beach,' she said.

James Murray's smile was one of relief. 'Ah yes, a clever chap. Knows what he's doing. And

I know what I should be doing. Your mother will be sending out a search party.'

He left them and after a few minutes a young girl appeared behind the bar looking rather surprised to be there. Had she been sent to keep an eye on things and report back, Nicole wondered? It was obvious Daniel's parents couldn't get away quickly enough and that hurt.

'So your mum and dad run a business too?' she said.

Daniel looked proud. 'They've been in this line for years, all the time I was growing up. They took this place over last year. There's spacious living accommodation too, which suits them. There's plenty of room there for me to make it my headquarters while I'm deciding what I'm going to do for the rest of my life.'

She nodded. She liked his parents. They were the right kind of people to make a success of anything, Nicole thought, so friendly and dynamic. Tactless, perhaps, but she couldn't blame them for making a mistake in her identity when Daniel hadn't kept them up to date.

He passed the menu across to her. 'What will you have?'

'That looks good,' she said, pointing. 'Red Thai chicken curry. I'd like that, please.'

'One of Dad's specialities,' he said. 'Good choice. I'll have it too.'

'I'm surprised to see there are other things beside fish on the menu.'

He smiled as he got up to order at the bar. He came back with two large glasses filled with colourless liquid. 'Lemongrass and ginger,' he said. 'Homemade this very morning I expect. It'll do for a start.'

'Made by your mother?'

'She's nothing if not inventive.' He sat down. 'Well now, tell me what you think. Has Adrian got it together or hasn't he?'

She smiled. 'Of course he has. It's impressive that he started with such a simple concept and has turned it into a successful way of life. Financially, I mean, as well as fulfilling. He had a dream and he went for it. I can see why you wanted Olaf and Pippa to see him at work.'

'Me too,' Daniel said, looking down at his hands on the table. 'I wanted it more than anything.'

She was silent. Well, what did she expect? No way was she going to let him know how this wounded her. 'Olaf's so different from your friend,' she said.

'But you like Olaf, don't you?'

'I expect most people do,' she said, more tartly than she intended. 'He sees his creations as works of art not to be sullied in the market place.'

'So why rent that shop in Trevillick?'

Nicole was silent. She had wondered that

too. Maybe it was something to do with proving something to his father.

'How long will it be before they realise that what they're doing is not enough?' Daniel leaned forward as if she needed convincing of something she had already seen for herself. 'They have to go all out to be a financial success. I wanted Olaf to understand that. Pippa now, she's different. I've hopes of Pippa.'

'Well, yes, but Olaf wasn't keen on her coming with you today. That means, surely, that he's no intention of being other than he is, laid-back and waiting for the spirit to move him.'

Daniel shrugged. 'I wish I could make him see that he must consider being more commercialised.'

'We can't change people however hard we try,' Nicole said. 'There's something strong about Olaf under all that dreaminess. And Pippa takes notice of her brother.'

'Adrian is passing on his vision to us all,' Daniel said. 'Because of it we feel wonder and admiration that lifts our spirits. But that's only because we've had the chance to see his work. People come for miles, you know, after checking the website.'

'Stonebalancing.com,' said Nicole thoughtfully. 'Flotsamfollies.com. Sounds good.'

'If it ever happens,' said Daniel.

Their food came. The curry was excellent and while she was enjoying it Nicole thought of those wonderful compositions from something as simple as boulders found on the beach. There was a meditative quality in watching Adrian at work. It felt wonderful

'Why can't we make mackerel curry?' she said.

Daniel looked startled. 'What?'

'I don't know why I said that. I was thinking of the stones and it just slipped out. Mackerel curry. Mundane, wouldn't you say, after all that wonder?'

He smiled. 'The subconscious mind is a wonderful thing.'

'Zelda and I need an alternative mackerel dish on the menu. Maybe for a different night of the week, that's all.'

He said nothing for a moment. He raised his glass to his lips and looked as if he were taking this seriously.

'Not a bad idea,' he said at last. 'While you're having your coffee here with Mum I'll slip backstage and see what I can find out from Dad.'

His mother brought the tray of coffee things in with her. Deftly, she poured and added milk.

'Such pretty mugs,' Nicole said as she took the one handed to her.

Felicity looked pleased. 'A local potter makes them for us from our own design. We

125

aim for a beach and sea theme.'

Nicole smiled. 'It's impressive. You have some good ideas.'

Felicity glowed at the praise and as Nicole sipped her coffee she thought how Daniel's mother seemed so much more approachable now she was seated with her at the table. She began to talk of the tourists and how some of them returned year after year expecting everything here to stay exactly the same. Nicole told her about Zelda's tearoom near the Dancing Hole on the headland and how she had come to Kenvarloe to help her aunt in her misfortunes.

The time passed pleasantly until Daniel returned. They left as some prospective customers entered, exclaiming at the decor.

'I hope the food's as good,' one of them said.

'Oh it is,' Daniel said as he held the door open for them. 'You can be sure of that. Highly recommended.'

Nicole giggled as they walked to the car. 'Biased, wouldn't you say?'

'True, though.'

He seemed in a light-hearted mood as they set out for home. They talked about his parents' restaurant and decided that Daniel might drop in at Kenvarloe Cottage tomorrow to see if he could adapt his father's recipe to include local mackerel.

It wasn't until they were nearing Kenvarloe

that Daniel raised the subject of the stone balancing again.

'Would you have a word with Pippa about it tomorrow?' he asked. 'You'll see her before I do and it might be better coming from you. I don't want to put her under any more pressure.'

It wasn't until Nicole was getting ready for bed that she wondered what pressure Pippa was under. She wished she had asked him.

With an ache in her heart Nicole opened her bedroom curtains for a last look outside over the intervening rough ground to the sea. She had done this every night since her arrival, hoping that the peace and beauty out there in the moonlight would ensure a good night's sleep.

Now she needed its healing properties more than ever. The day out with Daniel had been wonderful, but the strain of hiding her growing feelings from him was enormous.

Dusk had been falling as he dropped her outside the cottage door and with a friendly wave had driven off up the track, refusing her offer of refreshment. She couldn't tell if he glanced towards Pippa's home or not. She knew he would be thinking of her anyway, wishing that she had been with him so she could ask questions and understand how to set about making *Flotsam Follies* the financial success it deserved to be.

And because this hadn't been possible

Daniel had asked her to get her reactions to what she had seen across to Pippa instead. She would do her best, of course, and show Pippa the leaflet she had picked up from the display stand on the beach. Stonebalancing dot com, she thought, an easy enough website to remember. She didn't know if Pippa and Olaf owned their own computer and hadn't thought to ask.

She stretched and yawned. She was shattered, too, physically and emotionally. She thought of Daniel driving the few miles more to his camp site at Kalendra. There was no soft bed for him in a comfortable room with a handy bathroom nearby.

A feeling of concern for him swept over her as she thought of him crawling into his sleeping bag, exhausted with the miles of driving he had done in the car he had hired specially with a day out with Pippa in mind.

Sadly, she dropped the curtain into place and got into bed.

NICOLE MUST KEEP A PROMISE

By the time Nicole finished filling Zelda in next morning on all the events of the day in Lyme Regis, the hands of the kitchen clock had crept round to nine-thirty.

Zelda struggled up from the breakfast table.

'I promised to ring Mark before he started work.'

Nicole looked at her in surprise. Mark seemed a million light years away from what she had been describing, so that for a moment she found it hard to think who he was.

'Wake up, girl,' Zelda said as she reached for the phone.

'I'll dial for you,' Nicole said but before she could do so the ringing tone rang out.

Zelda's voice sounded full of concern and when at last she hung up she turned a troubled face to Nicole. 'There's a problem,' she said

Nicole had guessed as much. She felt breathless. There had been an accident, Daniel had lost his way to the campsite in the dark and hit a tree, and he was lying in a hospital bed somewhere unconscious . . .

Zelda gazed at the phone in its cradle on the kitchen wall as if it was solely to blame for what Mark had told her. 'Olaf turned up at the market garden yesterday evening looking for a job,' she said. 'I can't understand it.'

Whatever she had imagined, Nicole hadn't expected this. 'But that's crazy.'

Zelda sank down on her chair. 'It's true.'

Nicole was silent, trying to picture Olaf shovelling earth or painstakingly planting out seedlings with those long-fingered hands of his. Impossible.

Zelda, obviously doing the same, sighed. 'I haven't heard the van go out this morning, have you?'

Nicole shook her head and then got up and opened the back door to the freshness of the morning as if she could tell from here exactly what was going on in the cottage next door.

Zelda was clearing the table now, working quickly to compensate for having only one good hand. Her lips were pressed together and her shoulders drooped.

'I've only known them for six months,' she said. 'But they feel likc family.'

'So has Mark offered Olaf a job?'

'Not yet. He's wondering what to do about it. He's got problems of his own, you see. Olaf's going out there to see him again this morning.'

'Could you manage here if I offer to man the shop with Pippa?' said Nicole.

Zelda closed the cupboard door. 'Get yourself ready then, dear, while I pop round and suggest it.'

Nicole raced upstairs for her bag. By the time she got down again Zelda was back.

'There's no-one at home and the van's gone,' she said.

'Now what?'

'I'll ring Mark.'

Zelda took the phone off its stand, laid it on the worktop and dialled with her good hand. Mark took some time to come to the phone and when he did Zelda listened to what he had to say with frown lines creasing her forehead.

'Mark will try to get some sense into Olaf when he gets there,' Zelda said. 'There's a chance that he might drop Pippa off in Trevillick first, I suppose.'

'Let's hope so,' said Nicole. She felt like shaking the brother and sister for causing concern to Zelda. It simply wasn't fair when she had so much to contend with herself after the break-in and her accident.

She turned both taps on full and squirted washing up liquid into the bowl. She set to work vigorously. 'Why is it that the nicest people are the most annoying?' she said.

Zelda laughed but there wasn't much amusement in it. She straightened a tea towel on the rack. 'I can't answer that, dear.'

Nicole couldn't either, but by the time she had finished and emptied the bowl and rinsed out the mass of extra suds she felt a good deal calmer.

*   *   *

So much depended on the weather. That was the worst of relying mainly on casual walkers on the coast path catching sight of their notice board and on impulse heading their way. If it was too hot the numbers dwindled. Too cold and they stayed at home. But today, hot as it was, they were full to capacity for lunch. It was fortunate, Nicole thought, that one group opted to eat inside.

She spotted Don and his wife, Elise, from the group that had made a regular Saturday evening booking. They were seated at one of the picnic tables outside and looking round them with pleasure. It was good to see familiar faces.

'So,' said Don, leaning back in his seat as he waited for Elise to pour out. 'All set for Saturday night then?'

'Don't delay her,' said Elise. 'She has others to serve.'

'We're looking forward to Saturday,' Nicole said, smiling. 'I'll come and join you when things ease off a bit.'

It was good to sit down with them for a brief rest.

'So business is booming?' said Don. 'I admire your aunt coping as she does under difficulties. We've told one or two people about you.' He looked round with satisfaction. 'Some of them are here now.'

They were proving to be valuable friends and Nicole felt a rush of gratitude. 'That's good of you,' she said.

'Nonsense,' Don said. 'I've been in business myself and I know the score. You can't afford to stand still. New ideas all the time are what counts and an open mind to take them on board and act on them. Not like that place in town you were telling us about. The closed sign was on the door again when we were in Trevillick this morning.'

'*Flotsam Follies*?'

'That's the one. Paula was with us and she was champing at the bit because she wanted to buy something else. She was chuffed with that picture she bought for her grandson. She doesn't take kindly to being baulked.'

Nicole had a sudden vision of the lady in purple demanding the present that Olaf had given Zelda because it had taken her fancy. She wouldn't want to see Paula baulked either.

'I'll see to it that we have something here of Olaf's work to show her on Saturday evening,' she said, surprising herself even as the words left her mouth. 'Will Paula be coming with you this time?'

'We won't be able to hold her back,' said Elise.

'No gainsaying Paula in that mood,' said Don. He sounded rueful but his eyes were twinkling.

Nicole smiled. 'Good for her.'

Some of the other customers needed her attention now. She felt euphoric as she went to attend to them.

She didn't care what risk she had taken in promising something Olaf was sure to be furious about. She knew it was a good thing to do even if he didn't.

Zelda agreed in principle when she told her about it later. 'But I don't quite see how you'll manage to get Olaf to agree,' she said. 'Pippa might, I suppose.' She looked doubtful.

Nicole tried to sound confident. 'I'll work something out.'

The washing up was finished now and the kitchen cleared ready for the cream tea preparations.

'I'm going to put my feet up out in the shade with the newspaper,' Zelda said. 'There's not much to do now you've set the trays ready, Nicole dear. Feel free to go off for an hour or so if you like.'

Nicole was far too restive to join Zelda outside. Instead she headed off for the coast path, going south this time, away from Trevillick. The path descended for a while and then climbed steeply again. On her right the sparkling sea surged in and out and the sweet smell of gorse was pleasant.

After a while a mossy bank beneath an outcrop of rock looked too inviting to pass by. She sat with her hands round her bare legs and gazed out over the sea, deep in thought. She had promised something she knew Olaf would reject out of hand. Was she mad? But this was a golden opportunity whether he liked it or not and she wasn't going to pass it up even if she had to break into *Flotsam Follies* and steal the objects herself.

Or better still, offer to look after the shop on Saturday afternoon, suggest Olaf and Pippa go off beachcombing a long way away from Trevillick and insist they go straight home afterwards while she got the bus home to

Kenvarloe with her spoils.

She wouldn't mention the word spoils of course. But Saturday was likely to be a busy day here too. She couldn't sheer off and leave Zelda to cope on her own.

She pulled at a long piece of grass, found it wouldn't give and then abandoned it. No problem was insurmountable if you gave it enough thought.

Plan B? She had no immediate ideas on that one. Sneak up to *Flotsam Follies* when no-one was looking, smash the glass, climb in and gather as much as she could in a handy bin liner and then make her escape before anyone noticed what was happening? Dream on.

She gave a little giggle. It wouldn't help matters if she was clapped into gaol. Olaf, livid with rage, would refuse to visit her for sure and he wouldn't let Pippa either. Daniel would be too busy comforting Pippa to spare a thought for her. Only Zelda would come. And maybe Harriet.

The wave of longing that swept over her to see her sister took Nicole by surprise. She wanted Harriet to solve this problem for her as she had solved so many when they were growing up. As soon as she got back to the cottage she would ring her. And tell her what . . . that she was making idiotic plans to break and enter a shop in Trevillick and needed her big sister to hold her hand?

A stray cloud covered the sun and she saw

that others were drifting across the sky now. Gone was the bright warmth that had enticed her out onto the coast path. She got up and stretched before setting off back the way she had come.

*   *   *

Daniel, coming from the direction of the village with a loaded rucksack on his back, felt a mist of drizzle on his face that was pleasing after the heat of the morning. It wouldn't last, of course. Already the blue sky was spreading this way. But how was that? The sky stayed where it was, surely, while the clouds spread across the expanse of blue? Get your facts right, boy.

Olaf had surprised everyone, it seemed, by looking for work at the market garden and leaving poor Pippa on her own in the shop for a few hours. She hadn't got there until ten o'clock, which was late for opening up now it was high season. Muddled thinking on Olaf's part. How could it possibly help things if he had no time for beachcombing and making his creations? But nothing had come of his idea of working for Mark because Mark wasn't in a position to offer remunerative work.

Olaf's mood had been gloomy when he got back to *Flotsam Follies* and since his own presence there was no longer needed he had got the Kenvarloe bus instead.

Daniel walked down the track to the two cottages. As the rain cleared and the sun shone again the land and sea seemed rinsed in freshness. A lark rose from somewhere near and spiralled high in the sky above him.

There was no-one about. Pippa and Olaf were in Trevillick, of course. He walked up the path to the open door of Kenvarloe Cottage and went inside, calling as he went. The tearoom was empty and so was the kitchen. He dumped his rucksack on the floor.

Back in the hall he pressed the bell on the small table by the wall, but no one appeared. A burglar's paradise, this, he thought as he went outside again. At the back of the cottage in the shelter of the wall he saw Zelda asleep on a sun bed. He paused but it was too late. She had heard him.

She struggled up to a sitting position and looked round her, confused. 'It's been raining,' she said.

'Not much,' he assured her.

'I'm so sorry, Daniel. Have you come for a cream tea?'

'Don't disturb yourself. You look far too comfortable.'

'We had a busy lunchtime. Are you here to see Nicole?'

'I promised her my father's recipe for mackerel curry. I've brought most of the ingredients. I thought we might try it out.'

'What, now?'

He sat down at one of the picnic tables, ignoring the slight dampness. 'Shall I make us a cup of tea first?'

'You're a good boy. That would be wonderful.'

'You must promise to stay exactly where you are. If anyone comes I'll call you.'

In the kitchen he found all he needed and while the kettle boiled he unpacked his rucksack and laid the contents out on the worktop. Then, glancing up at the shelf above he saw four of Adrian Gray's cards arranged in a row. They looked good there, he thought, eye catching. He lifted one down to admire the quality of the print, reminded of Nicole's expression of wonder as she watched his friend perform his magic.

*   *   *

Nicole sensed something was different as she walked into the dimness of the cottage, blinking at the sudden change of light. She looked in wonder at the packets and bags lined up in the kitchen. Rice and red peppers, leeks, various herbs and some other things too. And one packet smelled suspiciously like mackerel. So Mark was here?

The kettle felt warm when she touched it and she saw that two mugs were missing from their hooks. She took another down and spooned in some instant coffee to make a drink for herself and then carried it outside to join the others on the patio.

Daniel sprang up from his chair. 'Nicole.'

A feeling of joyful surprise ran through her like the ripple of waves on the shore and her hand shook a little as she placed her mug on the table.

'Sit down, both of you, and we'll hear what Daniel has to say,' said Zelda.

Zelda looked comfortably relaxed as she leaned against the back rest of her sunbed, her mug of tea held carefully in her right hand. Not bad news then, Nicole thought as she did as she was told.

Daniel smiled at her, his eyes crinkling at the corners. 'I hope you'll be pleased,' he said.

'Has Olaf got himself a job?'

'Did you want him to?'

He looked so serious that for a moment she had the odd idea that her answer mattered a great deal to him.

'Hardly,' she said. 'What good would that be in the long run?'

'It would pay the rent,' said Zelda.

'For what, an empty shop?'

'My thoughts exactly.' Daniel drank his tea and put his empty mug down on the table, looked at it for a moment and then picked it up again. 'But I'm not here to talk about Olaf.' He drank the rest of his tea in one gulp.

Nicole smiled. 'But you are talking about him.'

139

'So I am. I can't seem to help it.' He frowned, put his mug down and pushed it to one side.

She studied his bent head with a sudden urge to stroke flat the wisps of fair hair that touched the collar of his navy sweatshirt. There was a sharp line of sunburn on his cheekbones. Memories stirred of the beach at Lyme Regis and the sun glancing down on them on as they viewed Adrian's mind-blowing creations.

'Nicole was telling me about your parents' restaurant, Daniel,' said Zelda.

He raised his head. 'That's why I'm here.'

'Oh, the mackerel recipe,' said Nicole. 'I see.'

'I've brought everything we need. D'you mind if I start on some preparation now to have it ready for later?'

He jumped up looking as eager as a schoolboy bent on some mischievous plan.

Zelda smiled up at him. 'I hope you'll make a lot so we can invite Pippa and Olaf to join us. Mark, too, if he's free? We need some guinea pigs to try it out.'

His eyes lit up. 'It'll be perfcct, I promise.'

'The sheer confidence of the boy!'

He grinned. 'A party's a good idea. I'd to talk to Pippa away from the gallery and you can have a go at Olaf, you two.'

'I wouldn't dare,' said Zelda.

'Not even for Olaf's own good?'

'Not even for that. We can't go about interfering in other people's lives to any great extent. It can never work.'

'But I interfered with yours, turning up on the doorstep,' said Nicole.

'That's not quite the same, dear.'

Nicole was silent, aware of the plans she was dreaming up for raiding *Flotsam Follies* and stealing a selection of Olaf's creations without him knowing anything about it. That would be interfering in a massive way.

'I think there's a good case for trying to help if you can see a way forward for someone and they can't,' Daniel said.

'You do?' Nicole looked at him gratefully, half-tempted to tell him of what she'd been planning. But no, she wouldn't do that. He was the official helper at *Flotsam Follies* and must be seen as trustworthy. In any case he might be dead against her doing anything as stupid as stealing some of Olaf's best pieces and bringing them here for their barbecue clients to pore over, for however good the reason.

'Off you go then, Daniel,' Zelda said. 'Nicole and I have something we need to talk about too.'

No prizes for guessing what, Nicole thought as she watched Daniel disappear round the side of the cottage. She wished she could follow him instead of discussing something she wished she'd never thought of in the first place. Next time she felt the urge to blurt out a promise she couldn't keep she'd have some sticking plaster handy.

'You don't think you've been too impulsive for your own good, dear?' Zelda said.

Nicole lifted her mug, smoothed the table where it had been and put it down again. 'Whatever possessed me to promise something I knew I couldn't do?' she said, her heart heavy. 'You're right, Zelda, as always. I'm going to have to come right out and make Olaf agree to let us have some of his stuff for Saturday, aren't I?'

'Use some of your charm on him.'

'For all the good that will do. Olaf's above that sort of thing. Maybe I should let you have a go. You've got oodles of charm, Zelda.'

Her aunt's dimple deepened as she smiled. 'I've got a feeling he's more likely to fall for yours.'

Nicole laughed. 'I've got as much charm as a bucketful of mackerel,' she said.

DISASTER AT *FLOTSAM FOLLIES*

Nicole had thought the meal outside this evening would be a repeat performance of the first one they had enjoyed together when she was just getting to know Olaf, Pippa and Mark. But not a bit of it.

This time the meal was more complicated

because it involved cooking rice indoors while the pan of delicious-smelling curry kept warm on the barbecue outside. There wasn't quite the smell of mackerel hanging on the air, either.

Earlier, when she had checked Daniel's progress in the kitchen, she had found him so engrossed with stirring his pan of simmering ingredients that when she spoke he almost let go of the spoon.

He turned a flushed face to her. 'You took me by surprise.'

'Sorry.' She started to back away.

'No, don't go. What d'you think of this?' He spooned a little of the mixture onto a plate. 'Taste that.'

It smelt so mouth-watering she could hardly wait for it to cool. 'It's fantastic, dreamy, out of this world . . .'

'Don't exaggerate, please.' He sounded disapproving, but his eyes were shining and she could sense his pleasure. She wanted to enthuse further, but he removed the spoon and turned the heat to low.

'It'll do there till the barbecue's hot and then we'll carry it outside.'

And that's what they did while Zelda got the pan of rice going on the cooker in the kitchen. While they waited for their guests to arrive Daniel tied a white tea towel round his waist and folded another into a mockery of a chef's hat and was ready to greet them.

'I'll take it off if any customers appear,' he promised as Mark came in to the garden followed by Olaf and Pippa.

'You think it would put them off their food?' said Mark.

'Not once they taste it,' said Nicole. 'It's wonderful.'

Once everyone was settled Daniel dished out a large plateful for each of them.

'Who would think mackerel curry could taste like this,' Zelda agreed when it was cool enough for her to pick up her fork and begin.

'So it'll go on the evening menu?' said Daniel as he sat down beside her.

'We'll have a special mackerel curry night every week,' she promised. 'Maybe Thursdays. What d'you think, Nicole? Will we do as well as this between us, d'you think, dear? We'll advertise it well, of course.'

Nicole laughed. 'We know who to employ as chef if we can't.'

Pippa was moving her rice around her plate and then left a heap of it on the side. She hadn't touched much of the rest of the meal, either. She looked down at it as if wondering what it was doing there.

'I hope we shall still be here in Kenvarloe,' she said. She turned anguished eyes on her brother that seemed to emphasise the significance of her words.

For a moment no one spoke. Then Mark cleared his throat. 'We certainly hope so,

Pippa.'

Zelda leaned towards Pippa and patted her hand. 'Oh my dear, you're not thinking of leaving us and moving on somewhere else?'

Her lips trembled. 'I . . . don't know.'

Olaf said nothing, but his lips tightened. There was something in his expression that made further questioning impossible. They all realised this and were silent for a long awkward moment.

Pippa, white-faced, looked down at her plate.

Nicole laid down her fork. 'Any hope of a second helping?' she asked in an effort to ease the tension.

Daniel had eaten his own plateful at record speed. 'Loads to be cleared,' he said. 'Come on, everybody, eat up.'

Pippa was out of her seat at once and moving to the barbecue. 'I'll do it,' she said. 'I like to help.'

She busied herself with serving first the rice and then Daniel's wonderful mackerel curry to all those who wanted more. Earlier there had been no difficulty in finding something to talk about. Now the atmosphere was strained as they struggled to find words to hide the underlying concern they all felt.

At the beginning of the meal Nicole had hoped that when they had eaten all they wanted she might take Olaf to one side and ask if he would let her bring some of his work back to Kenvarloe to have on display on Saturday evening. But that was now totally out of the question. Instead she commented on the recipe Daniel had written out for her earlier while Zelda made great play of holding her fork in her left hand and failing.

They fell silent again after that and the evening ended suddenly. What Daniel felt about not being able to talk to Pippa on her own as he accepted Mark's offer of a lift, Nicole could only imagine.

Zelda refused help from their guests in clearing up. 'I could see how shattered those poor dears next door were,' she told Nicole after everyone had gone and she and Nicole were viewing the remains of the meal. 'Mark too. It would have been cruel to make them help, don't you think, dear?'

'It was unkind of them not to tell us what it was all about,' Nicole said. She picked up the empty salad bowl.

Zelda looked desolate. 'I'll miss them if they go.'

Nicole stared at the bowl in her hands. 'Pippa said she hoped they'd still be here. That doesn't mean anything definite though, does it, Zelda? Are we jumping to conclusions here?'

'It was the way Olaf looked. And Pippa too.'

'Perhaps they'd had a row.'

Zelda looked horrified. 'With each other? Never.'

'Not if something serious was at stake?'

'But what could that be apart from *Flotsam Follies*, dear?'

Nicole was silent. She dare not think of any other reason because of her fear that it might involve Daniel. He had made no comment at the time about Pippa's remark. But neither had she. She began to stack the empty plates and collect the cutlery together.

'Leave it,' said Zelda. 'It's not important.'

To her dismay Nicole saw that her aunt's normal high colour had faded and her shoulders drooped. She pulled two chairs clear of the table. 'Let's sit for a while,' she said. 'It's not late. We need a rest.'

Zelda sank down with a sigh of relief

'Presently I'll soak all we can in the sink overnight,' said Nicole. 'I'll get up early tomorrow and see to it before breakfast. Promise.'

Zelda smiled. 'You're worth your weight in gold, Nicole. I mean it, dear. From next Saturday you'll be on a regular wage.'

'What?'

'You heard me, dear.'

'But no-one gets paid for going to prison.'

'You've more sense than to let that happen, I'm sure.'

'I'm not,' said Nicole, leaning back in her seat and staring over to the rocky headland. 'I have to do something and Olaf's not going to play ball, is he?'

'You'll manage somehow.'

'D'you mean I'll find a way to break in to *Flotsam Follies* and not get caught?'

'I've great faith in you, Nicole. I'm sure a way will turn up. Have I told you the legend of the Dancing Hole?'

'I don't think so.'

'The time to be up there on the headland is when the setting sun shines through the hole and the shadows of some of the lower boulders seem to be dancing as the sun gets lower in the sky. They say good luck comes your way if you do.'

'You've tried it out then, Zelda?'

Her aunt laughed and Nicole was glad to see some colour back in her cheeks. 'If I did it would be just before you turned up, Nicole dear. But that was just a lucky chance.'

'Well, it's too late for me now,' said Nicole, smiling. 'The sun's too low. I might try it tomorrow if the sky's clear. I could do with a bit of luck.'

Zelda smiled and got up from her seat. 'Bed now, I think, for both of us. We'll let the dew do its work on all this, shall we, dear?'

'The best idea you've had all evening,' said Nicole. 'Apart from the tale about the Dancing Hole, of course.'

*   *   *

The idea came to Nicole in the middle of the night. Great, brilliant, wonderful! She wouldn't

148

have to try out the magic of the Dancing Hole after all for inspiration. This was so simple she wondered why she hadn't thought of it before. Staying in bed wasn't an option after that. She pulled on her fleecy jacket, dragged a chair to the open window, pulled back the curtains and looked out.

In the distance she heard the murmur of the invisible sea surging against the cliffs. She smelt the salt in the air and imagined the breeze carrying it far inland and teasing the bracken that was beginning to brown as summer advanced.

She thought of Pippa, totally loyal to her brother even if her heart was no longer in the odd life they had chosen for themselves. Nicole knew that sometimes when Pippa and Olaf absented themselves from *Flotsam Follies* they were visiting their artist father in Newlyn and trying to convince him that purchasing their shop in Trevillick wasn't a good idea. Pippa had told her these things in confidence and so she couldn't give a hint of any of it to anyone else.

Tomorrow was Thursday, two days before Elise and Don and their group arrived for their mackerel supper expecting a selection of Olaf's work to be on view.

She smiled in the darkness, her heart light as she thought how easy the solution was without the need to involve anyone else. Those photos that Adrian had taken of his work were superb. She doubted whether she could match their quality when she photographed Olaf's but never mind, it would answer her purpose.

Back to bed now to be up bright and early tomorrow to get the chores done in record time. She would get the afternoon bus into Trevillick, no problem.

Her plan depended on *Flotsam Follies* being open for business, of course, and she hadn't taken that into consideration. She thought of it only as she boarded the bus the following afternoon. But even if Olaf and Pippa had taken the time off surely Daniel would be guarding *Flotsam Follies* for them?

She opened her bag to check that her camera was there as she knew it would be. She had also jotted down Daniel's mobile number in case the worst happened and *Flotsam Follies* was closed. They had probably given him a spare key.

She gazed out at the barren scenery and the blue line of sea in the distance, wishing the bus would get a move on instead of lumbering slowly round corners and coming slowly to a stop every now and again to pick up passengers.

Arriving in Trevillick at last, her heart quickened as she hurried up the cobbled street to the gallery. Although there was no harm in what she was going to do she felt like a criminal.

To Nicole's delight, Pippa was in sole charge at *Flotsam Follies* and so photographing the lovely things that Olaf had made was no problem at all. She was particularly pleased with the small boats with their bright sails.

'How are you getting home?' she asked Pippa when she had finished.

Pippa looked vague. 'The van, I think. Daniel went off with Olaf. They'll be back soon.'

Nicole glanced at her watch. 'I'll need to hurry to get these printed before the bus goes.'

'You could wait for Olaf and get a lift home with us.'

Nicole stuffed her camera in her bag and looked round in case she had forgotten anything. 'Better not. I'll feel too guilty. Don't tell Olaf I've been here, will you?'

'I'll say nothing about it,' Pippa promised.

The young male assistant at the phone and camera shop, recognising Nicole, came forward to greet her.

She produced her camera and removed the card. 'I need to print these, but I'm in a bit of a hurry.'

He smiled. 'No problem.'

'Five by seven, please.'

She craned forward so that she had a clear view of each print as it came out of the machine. Critical as she was of her work, she was pleased with the results.

She glanced at the clock on the wall as she paid for the service and saw that she had ten minutes to spare. Time to purchase some large sheets of coloured cardboard from the newsagent next door. Perfect. A job well done. Now she could have evidence of Olaf's work on display on Saturday. Members of the group could see what was on offer and if they liked what they saw could place orders for the pieces or for something similar. Even Olaf would be pleased about that.

To her dismay the bus was late. The misty headlands in the distance were fast disappearing into the background of lowering cloud. Things changed so quickly, she thought, remembering the bright harbour scene of the day she had arrived.

Now it looked merely gloomy and the moisture in the air was turning into drizzle. She pulled her jacket more tightly round her as she waited.

She wondered where Daniel and Olaf had gone today. Hopefully to sort something out, if that was possible and Olaf wasn't too proud to take advice.

Deep in thought, she didn't see the van as it pulled up a short distance away until she heard Olaf's voice calling to her that if she wanted a lift back to Kenvarloe she'd better be quick as they were holding up the traffic.

'What's that you've got there?' he asked

as she scrambled into the back behind Pippa, taking care not to crush her rolls of cardboard.

She felt herself flush as she fastened her seat belt, glad that Olaf accepted her mumbled reply that it was just something she needed. The prints were safely hidden in her bag.

No-one was inclined to talk and the atmosphere inside the van was as gloomy as the deteriorating weather outside. By the time they arrived at the track leading down to the cottages the rain was heavy.

With muttered thanks for the lift Nicole ran indoors, clutching her precious cargo to her in an effort to keep it dry.

*   *   *

Several people had turned up for lunch, but there were no takers for cream teas. Zelda was more concerned about Nicole's exploits in town than her own lack of takings on this rainy day.

'All done,' Nicole told her as she peeled off her jacket and hung it on the back of a chair in the kitchen. She removed the elastic band round the sheets of coloured card and spread the inside one out on the kitchen table, weighed down with four of the pretty stones from the beach that normally lived on the windowsill.

'Blue,' she said. 'I bought three different colours to show the photos off. Only the outside one got a bit wet. It'll dry. And there's a tube of extra strong glue.'

'And the photos?'

'Here they are.'

Zelda craned forward to look as Nicole slid them out of the folder. 'You took masses, dear. Well done!'

Nicole was glad that she had asked for the larger size, because in them every little detail of the wood that Olaf had used showed to advantage.

The photos that Nicole chose to display on the blue background made Zelda draw in a breath of delight. When she had stuck them in position Nicole carried it carefully into the tearoom and laid it on one of the tables. Any doubts that she had that the objects wouldn't photograph well were immediately dispelled.

By the time she had glued the remaining photos to the green and cream sheets she felt a glow of relief. She pressed the last print down with a soft tissue and then stood back to admire the effect, feeling almost as if the work in the photographs was entirely her own creation.

'They'll love them,' said Zelda, awed, as they took the third sheet in to the tearoom. 'I can't wait to get them up on the wall.'

Reluctantly it was agreed to leave this until Saturday afternoon in case Olaf came in and caught sight of them.

*   *   *

All that evening Nicole thought of those sheets of photographs with a secret glow of pride, imagining the orders pouring in for Olaf's work and his gratitude for her initiative. With luck every item he had made would be gone from *Flotsam Follies* because of it. Of course she had no idea what it was all worth, but surely it would help his finances and prove to his father that what he was doing was worthwhile? It might even convince his father to rent the shop to him instead of taking it over for his own work. Olaf would revel in his father's respect at last. She had the feeling that Olaf had rarely experienced that before.

The clouds had rolled away now to reveal a pale azure sky streaked with pink and orange towards the west. All of a sudden she wanted to be out there, breathing in the salt-fresh air.

'Feel like a walk, Zelda?' she asked.

'Not me,' said her aunt from the comfort of her deep armchair. 'The news'll be on in a minute.'

Laughing, Nicole left her to it.

As usual the sea called and she headed for the headland to climb up on the highest boulder to check if it was the right time of evening for the setting sun to shine through the aperture and make the others come alive. Almost, but not quite.

She settled herself to wait, glad she had

155

brought her waterproof jacket so she could sit on it in dry comfort. She wondered if, seeing the setting sun shining through the hole for the first time, she would want to dance and sing because she was alone and tomorrow might bring a change in Olaf's fortunes. With a buzz of anticipation she gazed at the aperture.

In her jacket pocket her mobile rang. She pulled it out and clicked it open, still with her mind on the sun that would soon be in the right position in the sky.

'Hi there, Nicole,' Bradley's voice said in the flat nasal tone she had come to know so well and that now sent a shudder through her heart.

She almost dropped the phone. 'Bradley?' she whispered.

'Guess what! I'm in Trevillick at this very moment. Could we meet up for a bit of a chat at the weekend, yes? Closure, you see. Are you up for it? I'll put Sandy on to talk to you if you like.'

Confused, Nicole was silent. Sandy? She glanced at the setting sun and then at the beam of light now streaking through the aperture. Viewing this was supposed to bring good luck not bad. The rocks blurred and then cleared again.

'Nicole?'

'I . . . don't know,' she said.

'Do come,' he urged, more warmth in his voice now.

For a moment she wondered if she were dreaming this. 'I must think . . .'

'We'll be at the Harbour Café on Sunday morning. See you there, yes?'

'Yes,' she repeated hardly knowing she had said anything, but aware that a momentous decision had been made. She had hardly thought of Bradley these last few days and now he was back on the end of her phone. But this time he sounded different and she had agreed to his suggestion.

Her euphoria about the photos vanished now along with the setting sun. She stood up and gazed down the coast towards Witten Head that looked strangely remote in the misty distance.

She had agreed to see Bradley and knew that she must keep her promise and trust that seeing him again would bring closure as he had promised. But for the moment she would put the phone call to the back of her mind and think only of the Saturday Group exclaiming over Olaf's creations and maybe changing his fortune in a way that would surprise him.

But as she walked slowly back to Kenvarloe Cottage in the gathering dusk, the image of Bradley's face insisted on intruding.

She let herself into the cottage and checked that Zelda was engrossed in a programme about dolphins that followed the news. She made coffee for them both.

'A nice walk, dear?' Zelda asked, her eyes

on the television screen.

Nicole placed the tray on the small table and sat down beside her. 'I was in the right place at the right time to see sunshine streaming through the hole,' she said.

'Then you're sure to have some good luck, dear.'

'I hope so.'

'You don't sound too sure.'

At any other time Nicole might have believed it, but not now. She sipped her coffee, deep in thought. She had become so immersed in the life here that Bradley's phone call had taken her by surprise. Now she regretted agreeing to meet him on Sunday.

The best she could hope for was that he would promise to leave her alone in future. They were meeting in a public place in Trevillick at his suggestion. She would feel safe there. There was no reason to believe he knew where she was now living.

'Well, who knows?'

Zelda swivelled round in her seat, looking anxious. 'You're all right, aren't you, Nicole dear. Your photos are wonderful. I'm sure Elise and Don will think so. Even Paula.'

'Paula too?' Nicole smiled.

The programme came to an end and Zelda clicked the TV off.

'Then that must be the good luck I'm looking for,' said Nicole.

She was glad she had the mackerel barbecue

tomorrow to think about. The colourful sunset tonight promised good weather to come and there were those three sheets of photos all ready to be viewed. If the good luck wasn't for her she could rejoice in it for the sake of Olaf and Pippa. Daniel would be pleased for them, too, if the orders came flooding in.

Daniel . . . her heart lurched as she thought of him. He had given so much of himself to help *Flotsam Follies*. Now if all went well, he would feel justified in giving his time and expertise. But then what? Was he already making plans to move on and complete the long distance walk he had planned or would he want to stay around longer for Pippa's sake?

Life was complicated.

*   *   *

After a disturbed night full of fragmentary dreams, Nicole fell into a fitful sleep as dawn was beginning to creep across the land. When she next woke the sun was shining through her curtains and she knew it was time to get up.

There was no sound from downstairs but she suspected that Zelda would be down there already making a start on the dough for the rolls because she liked to be well ahead in her preparations.

Nicole pulled on her oldest jeans and yesterday's T-shirt, planning to have a change of clothes after a shower later. She was reaching into the cupboard for the cereal packets when a police car came driving down the track. It pulled up behind Olaf's van and two policemen got out.

'Something's going on next door,' Zelda said, a worried frown creasing her forehead.

Nicole put the packets on the table and followed her outside. Olaf and Pippa emerged from their cottage looking stunned and anxious.

Zelda rushed out at once and took Pippa in her arms. Nicole, following, saw Olaf talking to the driver of the police car and then looking round vaguely as if not quite sure what he was doing here.

'It's the gallery,' Pippa sobbed. 'It's burnt.'

'There was a fire,' said Olaf.

'Nothing you can do, sir,' one of the policemen said. 'But you'd better be on the scene. We'll drive you.'

Olaf shook his head. 'We've got the van.'

Shocked, Nicole turned to stare after the police car as it reversed up to the road. *Flotsam Follies* destroyed? This was a nightmare.

Olaf, grim-faced, looked at his sister. It was plain he thought she was in no state to accompany him to town. 'I'll go on my own,' he said, feeling in his pocket for the keys. He seemed about to say something else, but then thought better of it.

In dignified silence he strode towards the

160

van that was parked as usual diagonally across the track. The vehicle started with a roar and he was off. Nicole watched it go, her heart sore.

Between them they got Pippa into their kitchen and sat her down at the table where she sat drooping with her long hair falling over her face.

'There, there, dear,' said Zelda. 'We'll soon have a hot drink made and you can tell us all about it.'

Pippa brushed her hair away from her face. 'There's not much to tell.'

Zelda lifted the telephone from the wall, laid it on the table and dialled with her free hand. Nicole knew she was phoning Mark. He would pass on the news to Daniel and between them they would support Olaf as best they could. Meanwhile, there was Pippa to think about. Nicole filled the kettle and plugged it in.

Pippa's eyes looked huge in her white face as she gazed up at them. 'What will happen now?'

Zelda, her lips pursed, shook her head, for once with nothing to say. Nicole shivered, unable to believe what had happened. Not knowing the extent of the damage was frustrating.

With luck some of the work might be saved. But it was no use dwelling on that now. The best she could do at the moment was to produce cereal and toast and hope that someone would eat it.

* * *

From the outside *Flotsam Follies* looked much the same apart from the broken glass in the window and burnt wood around the outside of the door. Inside was a blackened mess.

Daniel stepped in through the open doorway ahead of Mark and saw Olaf standing at the far end of the room looking like a piece of carved marble among the ruin of his work. The local fire fighters had done a good job dowsing everything and now the bitter smell of charred wood almost made Daniel choke.

'It started in the small hours,' Olaf said, his voice flat.

'Have you eaten today?' asked Mark.

Olaf shook his head. 'Food's not important. The insurance people said they'd phone back as soon as they could.'

Daniel nodded, relieved that Olaf had had the sense to phone the company before trying to clear up. 'Good thing I left my mobile here,' he said. 'They've got my number?'

Olaf nodded. 'One of the lamps might have been left on,' he said. 'The shade must have caught and it spread. All this wood . . .' His voice faltered to a stop.

Daniel nodded again There was no point on dwelling on the cause of the fire at the

162

moment. First things first. 'I'll wait here for you if you like, Olaf, in case the insurance people phone back,' he said. 'They can leave a message with me about when to expect them.'

Mark, understanding, nodded and took the protesting Olaf away. 'We'll be in the Harbour Café,' he said. 'Not far away. OK?'

When they had gone Daniel went down to the workroom and opened wide the window to get more air circulating. He saw that the fire had begun to get a hold down here, no doubt because of the stack of dry wood Olaf had stored on the stairs. It was all a sorry mess.

Upstairs again, he took in the full extent of the damage. Only blackened ash remained of the objects that had filled this place such a short time ago. Weeks of creative work destroyed in minutes.

Daniel stood in the open doorway and breathed in the early morning air, his heart heavy. There was no question now of Olaf proving anything to his father. His own help in supporting Olaf and his sister had all been a waste of time.

'I CAN'T BEAR IT ANY LONGER'

So shattered were they by all that had happened both Zelda and Nicole had forgotten for the moment that today was

Saturday with the group coming this evening for the mackerel barbecue.

By the time the pretence of breakfast was over, the colour had returned to Pippa's cheeks and although silent, she had calmed herself enough to insist she attend to the washing up of the three coffee cups they had used.

'I need to check my rolls have risen and are ready for the oven,' said Zelda. 'And I need to make more.'

Nicole busied herself with the preparations, knowing that Zelda would prefer to do the actual making of the rolls herself, but was prepared to stand by and do all she could to help.

'It's a lovely day,' Pippa said in surprise.

They had hardly noticed.

'Could you wipe the tables outside, Pippa?' Nicole said. 'We can sit out there while the next lot of dough rises.'

As soon as Pippa had found a cloth Nicole went to the phone and dialled Daniel's mobile. 'I can't bear it any longer, Zelda,' she said as she did so. 'We need to know what's going on.'

She could rely on Daniel to tell her, but wasn't surprised that at the moment there was nothing to report because he was alone in the shop keeping guard while Mark took Olaf off for some food. She didn't ask Daniel what state the place was in. She could imagine that only too well. His voice sounded odd.

'Are you all right, Daniel?' she asked in concern.

'Why shouldn't I be?' he said. *'Flotsam Follies* isn't mine.'

She hesitated at his bitter tone that was so unlike him. She wanted to say more but knew it wouldn't be wise at the moment because he didn't want to talk about it at this stage. The cruel blow had struck him hard.

She was thoughtful as she replaced the receiver, knowing how much Daniel considered himself involved in helping Olaf and Pippa. Not only that, but she knew that *Flotsam Follies* was important to him because its success helped heal the guilt he had carried round with him all these years.

She thought of his enthusiasm for making *Flotsam Follies* a success and the help he had given the project. He was a good, caring man. This would hurt him deeply for Olaf and Pippa's sake as well as his own. He would feel a failure even though that was far from the truth. Would he go on his way now that he could do little more to help?

While Pippa was busy Nicole checked that the tearoom was in good order because their customers this evening would be coming inside to view the photographs. With a heavy heart she spread the sheets of them out on the tables, found some drawing pins and began to fix them to the walls. She must keep her promise to have some of Olaf's work on show

165

even though it was little use now.

How eagerly she had prepared these sheets of photos yesterday evening and how different she felt about them now. It hurt her to see again the pretty sails for the boats that Pippa had made and the table lamps of strangely shaped wood that only Olaf's creative imagination had made possible. Talented Pippa had fashioned exactly the perfect lampshades to suit them. The display of boats against the painted beach scene background looked charming too. Now all that was gone.

When she had finished Nicole stood back for a last check and then walked across to the window. Pippa had finished wiping the tables and chairs and was standing with her back to her staring out to sea. Was she wondering how soon Olaf would want to move away from Kenvarloe and leave the devastation of his dreams behind him?

Zelda was distressed, too, at the thought of losing the young neighbours she had come to love. Nicole hurried back to the kitchen and gave her a warm hug.

'What's that for?' said Zelda, her face flushed from bending down to reach in to a low cupboard for another baking tray.

Nicole smiled as she released her. 'Just for being you and to say I love you.'

'Me too,' said Zelda and then laughed at herself because her words had come out wrong. 'But now I must find something else for Pippa to do to keep her busy. Myself, too. I don't want time to think just yet.'

*　　*　　*

Mark arrived at lunchtime to find several customers sitting at the tables outside in the sunshine. Nicole, busy serving ploughman's lunches, waved to him.

'Come and have lunch, Mark,' she said. 'Zelda won't be long. She's gone back to Pippa's cottage with her to sort some things out.'

Concerned, Nicole noticed how weary he looked as he sat down heavily at an empty table.

She checked that everyone had what they wanted, produced a bill and took the money from a couple ready to leave. Then she was ready to serve Mark.

'I'm not really hungry,' he said, wiping his hand across his forehead. 'I'm due back at *Flotsam Follies* to relieve Daniel for a bit.'

She sat down opposite him. 'Is it that bad?'

He nodded. 'Couldn't be worse. The insurance people are due to phone again this afternoon to arrange a visit and Olaf's insisting on waiting at the shop to speak to them on Daniel's mobile. I don't know the ins and outs of everything, but it doesn't look good. Daniel's a tower of strength but it's all pretty hopeless.'

'I'll get you a coffee,' she said.

By the time she returned with a plate of sandwiches and two mugs the last of the customers was ready to move.

Mark ate slowly, engrossed in his own thoughts.

'You're a kind girl, Nicole,' he said at last.

She smiled. 'I try to be.'

'Zelda is so fond of you. She wouldn't want to move away from Kenvarloe and leave you here on your own, you see, not with that worry you have hanging over you.'

Nicole thought of Mark giving her a lift home from Trevillick the first time she had visited *Flotsam Follies* and telling him her fear of Bradley's phone calls.

'He wants to meet me,' she blurted out. 'He phoned yesterday. He's in Trevillick with a friend this weekend.'

'Ah.' Mark's eyes flickered. He sat up straight. 'And will you?'

'He said it would be closure. He seemed to mean it.'

'Maybe a good idea if you can bear to see him again?'

She moved his empty plate onto the tray and then stared at it. 'I think I will.'

'And Zelda? What does she think?'

'I don't want to worry her.'

'No.' He was silent for a few moments.

She had the feeling that there was something important on his mind that he was reluctant to share. She leaned forward, opened her mouth to speak and then closed it again. What right had she to question him? But she was deeply attached to Zelda and it seemed likely that it had something to do with her.

'You said that Zelda wouldn't want to move away and leave me here on my own?' she said after a struggle with herself.

He looked troubled. 'I care deeply for her. She knows that.'

'And she for you?'

He nodded.

Nicole took a deep breath, aware she was treading on delicate ground here. She remembered all too clearly what Zelda had once said about interfering in other people's lives.

'And you want to be together?' she said.

'I've long wanted it,' he said simply.

'Then I'm not going to stand in your way.'

He smiled, but his eyes looked sad. 'Zelda has a will of her own beneath all that sweet kindness, you know. She won't see you harmed.'

'She wouldn't really give up Kenvarloe Cottage and the teashop?'

'There's no need. I wouldn't want her to do that. I'd think of buying her a small car. My place is bigger, more of a home for the two of us and I must live on the premises.'

Nicole nodded. She could see that made sense. If it weren't for her broken wrist Zelda could travel daily, but that would heal in time. The only problem preventing this plan was herself and no way was she going to have that. She was determined, too, as much as Zelda.

'I won't have a problem for much longer once I get Bradley sorted once and for all,' she said. This was the motivation she needed to crush any lingering doubts that it was the right thing to do.

He looked up. 'You really mean that?'

'Never more certain.'

Mark looked more animated now. 'You won't be on your own, Nicole,' he said. 'I'll be on your case, keeping guard. When and where have you arranged to meet this man?'

'At the Harbour Café. Masses of people congregate round there, so I'll feel safe.'

Mark nodded his approval. 'A good choice. You won't have anything to worry about, I promise. Ah, here's Zelda now. Our secret?'

'Our secret,' Nicole said, smiling.

*   *   *

Daniel phoned late afternoon. At the sound of his voice Nicole's heart quickened.

'Nothing to report really,' Daniel said. 'But I knew you'd be anxious to hear from us. How's Pippa?'

She told him what little she knew, that Pippa had been helping Zelda get everything in place for this evening and had even made a batch of rolls herself. She had been withdrawn and silent, though, obviously worried about *Flotsam Follies* and their immediate future.

In return he told her that Olaf and been given the go-ahead to clear up the mess after the fire and that his father had called in briefly, taken a look round and then gone again.

'Apparently he had made himself responsible for the insurance premium on the items that Olaf made,' Daniel said. 'He was livid that Olaf hadn't kept a list of his stock and has no idea what it was worth. He frightened the living daylights out of me, I can tell you. I can't really blame him for being angry. Anyway Olaf's on his way home now.'

'I'll tell Pippa,' she said.

When the evening finally arrived Nicole found that for a time she was able to push the events of the day to the back of her mind and concentrate on the job in hand.

Zelda had dressed in her green frilly blouse and black skirt for the occasion and welcomed their customers with a smile. Pippa had gone home to be with Olaf and there was no sign of life from their cottage. She couldn't begin to imagine what was going on there and wouldn't think about it until later.

Elise and her husband, Don, introduced everyone. They found places to sit, exclaiming at the beauty of the evening and the view of the sea. They had come along the coast path from the south this time, and that was a relief. There was no talk of the fire at *Flotsam Follies* because they hadn't yet heard about it. And no mention either at the moment of the availability of Olaf's work.

'You won't remember all these people,' their friend, Paula, boomed. 'A different lot from last week. Except me, of course.'

She looked round proudly and pulled off her fleece to reveal a low-cut top decorated with so many sequins that Nicole was dazzled.

Soon the smell of sizzling mackerel filled the air. Nicole brought out the bowls of salad and then helped Zelda serve the rolls. She had already placed jugs of fruit punch on the tables.

It seemed that the simple menu was as popular as it had been the week before. Afterwards they leaned back in their seats while Nicole served coffee and biscuits.

'No more to eat for me,' Paula puffed, patting her midriff.

'When are we going to see those lovely items you promised to show us?' asked Elise.

Nicole paused. The moment had come. She got to her feet, glanced at Zelda and saw her smiling in encouragement, although she sensed a slight wariness about her.

'There's good news and bad news,' said Nicole. 'We've got a photo display inside of all the lovely things that Olaf made. I expect some of you would like to take a look in a minute. Maybe a few at a time?'

Paula struggled out of her seat. 'Lead on,' she said, making for the door.

'And the bad news?' asked Don quietly as several others followed her.

Nicole bit her lip. 'There was a fire during the night at *Flotsam Follies*.'

'A fire?' said Elise in alarm. 'Was anyone hurt?'

'Fortunately no one was there,' said Nicole. She clutched the back of a chair to steady herself as the enormity of it all hit her afresh. Olaf's dreams, and Pippa's too . . . all gone.

Don looked serious. 'I see,' he said.

'You mean everything's destroyed, all the things he made?' said Elise.

'We're afraid so,' said Zelda.

'That's terrible. He must be shattered. But he can make more?'

Nicole shook her head. 'There's a lot to consider.'

At that moment they heard the sound of footsteps and Olaf appeared round the side of the building. He looked stunned at seeing they had company. Pippa, following, threw Nicole an anxious glance.

Zelda sprang up, scattering cutlery. 'Olaf!' she cried. 'Oh, poor dear, are you all right? What happened? Come and sit down, and Pippa too.'

Looking dazed, Olaf did as she said.

Pippa hesitated. 'Is there anything I can do to help?' she asked. 'I'm sorry I wasn't here earlier.'

Zelda, making soothing noises, poured them each a glass of fruit punch. 'Have you eaten? There's plenty left.'

'Olaf forgot you'd have company tonight,' Pippa said. She swallowed hard.

Don and Elise looked at them with sympathy.

'Zelda told us about the fire,' Elise said. 'We're so sorry.'

Olaf drained his glass in silence. Nicole wished him anywhere but here, afraid all the time that Paula and the others would soon come bursting out and making things infinitely worse with enthusiasm for his creations that no longer existed.

'I think we should be thinking of making a move,' said Don.

Zelda looked distressed. Nicole knew how much she wanted to be alone with Olaf and Pippa to give them what comfort she could. At the same time she was concerned that Don and Elise's group shouldn't feel they were being hustled off when they were enjoying themselves.

There was a clamour of voices. Paula and the others appeared carrying with them the sheets of photographs.

Paula smiled with supreme confidence. 'I hope you don't mind us taking them off the wall? We can look at them better out here. So clever to choose these background colours to display your lovely photos.'

She spread the sheets out on the tables and everyone gathered round. Nicole glanced at Zelda and shrugged. The situation was out of her control now. She had thought she was doing such a clever thing that would please everyone, but it had back-fired in a way she hadn't anticipated.

In a daze she heard Don explaining the circumstances to those who hadn't already heard.

Olaf got to his feet. 'May I look?' he said.

A PARENTAL INFLUENCE

The way was made clear for him and in the sudden silence Nicole's mouth felt dry. Olaf appeared to grow in height and his pallor frightened her. He looked hard at the photos. Pippa moved to stand beside him.

He turned to his sister. 'You knew about these?'

She nodded. 'I thought . . . They won't do any harm, will they?'

Zelda half-rose in her seat as if she expected an angry reaction from Olaf. Instead he moved to the next table where Paula had spread out the yellow sheet of photographs. He bent to examine them and a lock of hair fell across his face.

175

As he pushed it back and looked up Nicole saw that his eyes had lost their deadpan expression and he was smiling. Seeing his lost work like this hadn't worked a miracle, had it? She gazed at him in wonder as she realised that it might be so.

'Great work, Olaf,' said Paula. 'Are you taking orders?'

'Please do,' said one of the others.

Olaf shook his head, but his smile didn't fade.

'But those dinky little boats are lovely,' said Paula. 'And that windmill.'

'I like the chair made out of driftwood,' said another. 'I'd like to order four of them for the garden.'

Olaf didn't appear to hear any of this. He stood up straight, looking younger and more approachable. 'I'd like to borrow these photos if I may, Nicole,' he said.

'But I want to have another look,' Paula objected.

Don got to his feet. 'Leave it, Paula,' he said. 'There's something going on here, and the poor chap's in shock. Next time perhaps.'

Elise started to gather her belongings. 'We've had a great time,' she said. 'Thanks, Zelda. You've done us proud again. Same time next week? I'll be in touch with final numbers.'

Even Paula could see it was time to go. She glanced at Olaf, saw he was examining the prints again and gave in with a sigh.

When they had gone Pippa drew her brother's attention to the photo of a model of a strange bird on the cream-coloured sheet of cardboard. It was the one that Olaf had made from the bent piece of driftwood she had found at Witten when they had gone to see the bird enmeshed in the fishing net.

'I liked that bird,' she said.

Olaf moved his fingers over the photo. 'No-one's ever seen a bird like that.'

'Or will again,' said Pippa sadly.

'It wasn't one of my best.'

'But I liked it.'

'Nothing can match the real thing. I was a fool to try.'

Nicole, gathering plates and glasses, was surprised at the lightness of his tone.

'Will you make me another one day?' Pippa said.

'One day,' he said. 'Not a Great Northern Diver because you don't normally see them round here. One of the other seabirds that I can model from life. If I'm lucky. I've been waiting to hear. Daniel will know soon. He's been setting things up.'

He wasn't making much sense here, but shock could do strange things to people, Nicole thought as she joined Zelda in the kitchen.

'That's most of it cleared,' she said. 'I'll see to the barbecue in the morning when I've done the washing up.'

Zelda looked anxious. 'Are Olaf and Pippa all right out there?'

'I think so. They're still looking at the photos.'

'Poor boy,' said Zelda sadly

'Poor Pippa too.'

'She wants what's best for Olaf, dear. He's the one needing help. I only wish I could give it. Mark should be here. Daniel too.'

'They're doing their bit at *Flotsam Follies*,' Nicole reminded her.

Zelda rubbed her hand across her face. 'I'll go and see if there's anything I can do.'

Left alone, Nicole put the coffee back in the cupboard and straightened the cloths on the rail. Then she followed Zelda outside and collected the spare cushions from some of the seats to carry indoors.

With her arms full she walked round to the other side of the cottage.

'So where is he?'

Nicole looked with amazement at the man who had appeared so suddenly. Sturdy and broad shouldered, his curly auburn hair greying a little at his temples, he seemed like a belligerent giant from another world. Impossible to believe that he had unfolded his huge frame from that low red sports car she could just glimpse parked behind Olaf's van.

'Are you looking for someone?' she asked.

'My son, Olaf. Have you seen him? Laurie Williams. You must be Nicole. I've heard about you.' He moved towards her and took her hand in a firm grip so that the cushions slipped and would have fallen if he hadn't rescued them.

She took them from him and put them down on a patch of grass. 'Olaf and Pippa are in the garden with Zelda,' she said.

'Ah yes, Zelda.' His voice boomed out in the quiet evening air. Paula could have taken lessons from him, she thought.

'I need to see my son,' he added more quietly. 'I could be the bearer of good news.'

'I'll show you the way.'

But he had his back to her now, looking towards the sea and the distant headland. She left him there and found Zelda talking to Pippa while her brother still examined the photos. They all looked so absorbed that Nicole hesitated to disturb them. But who knew, she might well find herself turned into a standing stone like one of those pillars on the moor if she didn't obey Olaf's father immediately. She wasn't going to risk that.

'Olaf,' she said. 'Your father's here.'

Startled, he looked up.

There was movement behind her as Laurie Williams came into view. Pippa jumped to her feet. 'Dad!' She flew to him and was enveloped in a huge hug.

'How's my downtrodden daughter?' he said, releasing her.

'Oh Dad, it's all gone, all Olaf's work.'

'And don't I know it?'

Her father's vibrant personality seemed to fill the air around him and Nicole felt as if she had faded into the background. Even Zelda looked subdued.

He strode to the table. 'What's that you're looking at, son?' he asked.

Olaf got to his feet awkwardly, looking thin and pale beside his father.

'Nicole took some photos. You can see for yourself, Dad, that I didn't waste my time.'

Laurie Williams peered down at them and then beamed approval. 'Excellent, my girl. I see you've got a sensible head on your shoulders which is more than I can say for these two.'

'That's not fair,' Zelda said.

He turned to her. 'We've met before, but you won't remember me. I'm the father of these two.'

'I can see that,' said Zelda with a glimmer of a smile.

He looked pleased. 'Not many people see a likeness.'

'I know them so well, you see.' Zelda's dimple deepened.

Nicole looked at her in surprise. Was Zelda flirting with him? But perhaps she really did see something in Olaf and Pippa that she recognised in their father, too. Some deep creative urge, perhaps, that manifested itself in different ways but was the same deep down.

'They've told me a lot about your niece and I can see for myself what an asset she is,' he said.

Nicole felt warmth flood her face. 'Taking some photographs seemed a good idea at the time.'

'A digital camera?'

She nodded.

'Then may we download them on computer?'

'Of course. But where . . .'

'Pippa should know what to do after all that tuition the young lad gave her. He set up a website, I hear, and spent hours showing her how to cope.'

'Well yes,' Pippa agreed. 'Daniel tried to teach me but . . .'

'Daniel did?' said Nicole. With a rush of relief she remembered the long hours he had spent with Pippa and how she had agonised about that.

'He was very patient,' said Pippa, unhappily. 'He wanted me to understand, but it's all so complicated.'

'Never mind that now,' said her father. 'I'll do it at once, then save them and print them out instead of taking these. You've got the printer set up?'

Pippa seemed to wilt under his scrutiny and Nicole felt a spasm of pity for her even though she was still thinking of what she had just heard. She should have had the sense to

181

realise that Daniel had to get Olaf and Pippa computer-wise. Not that Pippa would take to technology with any ease, she thought. She would much rather be out beachcombing or making her lovely fabrics. But there wasn't a lot of hope of her being able to do that now. Unless . . .'

'You said you had some good news, Mr Williams,' she reminded him

'Laurie.' He smiled broadly at her. 'But not as good news as this. You're a clever girl, Nicole, making a record of *Flotsam Follies*' stock so we've got proof of what was there for the insurance people.'

Nicole felt herself flush again, aware of how undeserving she was of praise. It hadn't occurred to her for one minute that a photographic record would be a useful thing to have.

'My solicitor will be happy,' said Laurie triumphantly.

'Can we offer you some refreshment, Mr Williams?' Zelda asked.

'No, no, my dear, I won't intrude. I just came to tell my boy that the Bird Sanctuary people are interested in seeing him again. Good thing you gave them my number. They've been trying to get hold of you.'

Olaf stared at his father. 'They have?'

'They want you down there again tomorrow, lad, so see you get there. We'd better get going now, if Nicole here will trust us with her precious thingummy card for a short while we can copy those photos?'

'Of course I will,' she said. 'My camera's upstairs.'

She ran to get it and then extracted the card and handed it to Pippa.

'We'll take good care of it,' Pippa promised.

They were anxious to be off now, the three of them, and when they had gone Zelda sank down onto a chair in the kitchen. Her usual colour had drained away and she looked exhausted.

Nicole looked at her in concern. 'I'll get the kettle on. I think we need something after all that.'

'A few shocks there,' Zelda agreed.

'Laurie Williams is dynamic, wouldn't you say?' Nicole could still feel the pressure on her hand from his strong grip.

'Olaf's always been keen on his bird-watching. I don't know what's going to happen now.'

'Or how it will affect Pippa.'

As she made coffee Nicole thought of the girl she was beginning to know well. She was such a support to her brother at *Flotsam Follies* and it seemed likely that it would now be taken from her.

She carried the mugs to the table and sat down.

Zelda picked up her coffee mug, took a sip and then put it down again. She tried to smile.

'You were the star of the evening, my love. I was proud of you.'

'I didn't deserve it, though, did I, with my ulterior motives?'

'But it paid off in a way you couldn't imagine.'

'Paula and the others will be disappointed if Olaf moves. It's all such a mess.'

Zelda sighed. 'We might be able to persuade him to make the things they want before he goes.'

'I suppose Pippa will go with him?'

'I don't know, dear. Maybe she'll stay with her father here and find something to do locally.'

'Like helping to run a tearoom with special mackerel evenings if you decide to leg it from Kenvarloe?'

Zelda looked at her in alarm. 'What's Mark been saying to you?'

'I've got eyes in my head, Zelda,' Nicole said gently. 'Even if he hadn't let something slip I would have known. In any case, I won't be here forever and what then?'

Zelda was silent but her cheeks were flushed. Nicole looked at her, her heart full. Her aunt hadn't had an easy time these last few years and she deserved some happiness now.

'Dear Zelda, I want the best for you and always will,' she said.

'You're a good girl, Nicole,' Zelda said

huskily. 'I promised I'd look after you at this difficult time, and so I will.'

'I know that,' said Nicole. She looked at her coffee, wondered why she had made some for herself when she didn't really want it, got up and poured it down the sink.

'I'll take mine up with me,' said Zelda. 'It's been quite a day.'

Sleep seemed impossible after all that had happened in the last few hours. At last Nicole could bear lying wide awake in the dark no longer. The clearing up downstairs needed doing and she could be getting on with it. Anything was better than dwelling on the thoughts whirling in her head.

Downstairs, she set to work first in the tearoom, straightening the tables and chairs and pinning the sheets of photographs back on the walls because she didn't know what else to do with them.

That done she moved to the kitchen, appalled at the state they had left the place in. But Laurie Williams' explosive appearance had put everything else from their minds and when he had gone they were both so exhausted that bed was the sensible option.

She was glad to have something to occupy her mind. By the time she had washed and dried everything she felt a great deal more relaxed. She wiped the worktops and hung up the cloths to dry and then opened the back door to look outside.

Moonlight shimmered on the roof of Olaf's van and she could still glimpse his father's car behind it. The cottage next door was in darkness. A peaceful scene and one that was now so familiar to her she felt as if she had been living here for months instead of weeks. But soon it was about to change and Daniel would need to return to his accountancy work in Lyme Regis.

Suddenly a great emptiness filled her. Hardly knowing what she was doing she grabbed a towel from the hook, went out, closed the door behind her and followed the moonlit path round the side of the cottage to the paved area on the other side. The picnic tables, filled so recently with a happy band of walkers enjoying the food and the company, now stood empty in the silvery light.

She put her towel down on the nearest seat and sat down. Then, leaning on the table with her head on her arms she let the tears flow. Daniel would go on his way and she couldn't bear it. His wish to give help where it was needed had come to nothing. He would carry his guilt at that long ago mishap in Crete with him for the rest of the way.

Daniel's belief that places like remote coastlines help give people a different perception on viewing their lives was now her belief too and she must hold to it. From the first, she had found peace in climbing up on the headland rocks to the Dancing Hole.

Olaf and Pippa found joy in beachcombing and the imaginative creation of objects from natural sources. Perhaps unconsciously Paula and her friends' spirits were touched by this. Lots of others were drawn to natural places too like climbers and ramblers. Others went camping, bird-watching and a million other things as well.

Daniel had talked about the natural world as the refuge of the spirit and now she began to understand a little of what he meant. She hoped that Daniel's love of the natural world would be his solace now.

She felt in her jacket pocket for her precious shell and ran her fingers over its smooth surface. Knowing Daniel had given her the strength to do what must be done.

Zelda had been her strength and support when she had needed it and now she would encourage her to follow her heart. Zelda could go off to the ends of the earth with Mark and live happily ever after. Nicole smiled as she tried to imagine this happening, Then she sat up and wiped her eyes. A market garden on the other side of Trevillick with Mark was Zelda's dream. Her teashop too.

She could help her keep that going for her as long as Zelda was happy for her to live here alone. And Zelda would be happy about that when she had sorted everything out with Bradley.

With new resolve Nicole stood up and

took a deep breath. She took a last look at the headland outlined against the glimmering water and then went back to bed.

*   *   *

Sparkling sea beyond the harbour wall and the cry of swooping seagulls filled Nicole's heart with optimism the next day as she sat at a table outside the café where she had agreed to meet Bradley. The tide was out and several of the boats left there by the receding water were resting on their sides on the hard sand. Several young boys ran among them shrieking and she smiled to see them.

She was deliberately early because she felt this would give her an advantage because she would see Bradley coming towards her before he saw her. Outwardly relaxed, she leaned back in her chair to wait. This might have been any sunny Sunday morning except that she was here in Trevillick and not helping Zelda at Kenvarloe. To her surprise Zelda hadn't questioned her decision to get the bus into town this morning. Maybe she thought she had arranged to meet Daniel.

Already the place was filling up. It was good to see so many holidaymakers enjoying the sunshine and providing cover and support for her even if they didn't know it.

On the table in front of her was the glass of orange juice she had ordered. What had she to be afraid of in this bright and happy place? She lifted her glass and took a sip, hoping that now the important moment was approaching she appeared totally at ease.

She put her glass down again and glanced about her. There was no sign of Mark, but he had promised to be near at hand just in case she needed assistance. With a beat of her heart she saw Daniel instead, walking towards her and turning his head to glance down at someone at his side.

But no, he wasn't Daniel.

Daniel didn't wear long red shorts or sleeveless yellow vests. This wasn't Daniel though he looked a lot like him.

She stood up. 'Bradley?'

He stopped suddenly and looked at her with a diffident smile that didn't quite reach his eyes.

'Hello there, Nicole,' he said in the flat tone of voice she remembered so well and which still sent a chill through her.

He glanced down at the petite dark-haired girl accompanying him. Her face was expressionless as she stared hard at Nicole.

'Sandy,' Bradley said. 'Meet Nicole. This is the girl I've told you a lot about.'

His tone indicated that what he had said hadn't been entirely good. This wasn't surprising, Nicole thought as she sank down again on her chair. She had done her utmost to make her position clear to him in the weeks before she moved down here and definitely wouldn't have been at her best.

'Hi,' Sandy said, her voice hard. She pulled out a chair as if she meant business and sat down. She had an aura of confidence about her that was disturbing.

Nicole swallowed, her mouth dry. She longed to take a sip of her juice, but felt it would be impolite. She must concentrate on getting through this meeting with dignity.

Bradley sat down too and beckoned to the girl who had served Nicole earlier. Ignoring him, the dimple deepened in her chin as she smiled at one of the other customers and handed him a newspaper before going back inside.

He gave an explanation of annoyance. 'Such bad manners, but what can you expect? But you don't want anything to drink do you, Sandy, in a place like this? I see Nicole's well provided for.'

'And why not?' said Nicole with spirit.

'Why not indeed if your standards are low.'

'I don't think we need to worry about standards as we won't be here long.'

He looked sullen. 'You agreed to meet.'

'I did indeed, Bradley, and here we are. Closure, you said. Sounds a good idea to me, in fact a brilliant one.'

'Sandy and I are getting married.'

Nicole let out a breath of surprised relief tinged with unexpected sympathy for Bradley.

But who was she to judge? She smiled with true warmth. 'Congratulations, both of you. I'm delighted to hear it.'

Sandy frowned. 'So I want no more of your pestering my fiancé, do you understand?'

Nicole gaped at her. 'Are you serious?'

'Never more serious in my life. So leave him alone in future.'

'Now, Sandy . . .' Bradley began. A flush spread across his face and he moved awkwardly in his seat.

Nicole smiled at him. 'I think we both know how it was back there in London, don't we Bradley? But not any longer, OK? I have your word for that?'

She was proud of her tone of voice, slightly amused, but full of confidence as if she were totally in control of the situation. As perhaps she was. Bradley had made her life a misery over a period of weeks, but he must have felt something for her or he wouldn't be here now. It was plain that this was none of Sandy's doing. She was now sitting on the edge of her chair, drumming the fingers of her right hand on the table.

Nicole smiled. She knew she could afford to look kindly on Bradley and put it all safely behind her. She had nothing to lose and everything to gain.

'OK,' he said. He smiled a little uneasily and then turned to check his appearance in the glass of the window behind him.

She wondered how she could have mistaken Daniel for him in the first place. It was true that there was a slight physical resemblance between them because of their broad shoulders and fair hair, but that was all. She couldn't imagine Bradley leaping into deep water to rescue her mobile. But of course the tide was out today so there was no need.

Bradley smoothed back his hair. He was trying too hard to impress, she realised, but surely this was unnecessary when he had his hard-bitten Sandy in tow?

'I just wanted to see you once more to say goodbye, Nicole,' he said. 'And to give you this.' He thrust a small polythene-wrapped packet at her.

She took it and saw at once that it contained the shell bracelet she thought she had lost. 'Where did you get this?' she asked in surprise.

The young girl waitress approached their table, pad and pen in hand. 'Is there anything I can get you, sir?'

'Nothing,' said Sandy. 'We're not staying. We've said all we've come to say.'

She got up and pushed her chair back so roughly that it knocked against the girl's hand. Her pen fell to the ground and rolled under the feet of a passerby and landed in the gutter.

The girl's hand flew to her face. 'Oh!'

'I'll get it,' said Nicole. As she retrieved it she saw that it was a pretty silver pen engraved with a design of intricate lines.

192

The girl smiled at her. 'It's a special one,' she said. 'Thank you. I couldn't bear to lose it.'

'So why not take better care of it?' said Bradley.

Nicole felt suddenly downcast. She looked down at the bracelet he had returned to her knowing she would never wear it again. This meeting was a waste of time.

Bradley could have told her of his engagement over the phone. He could have apologised to her for coming on too strongly in the past and indicated that he wouldn't trouble her again. He could have asked for her address so he could return the bracelet and she could have told him not to bother. Far better that way than to blight the beauty of the summer morning and leave her feeling unaccountably depressed.

'That's it then?' she said, preparing to leave.

Bradley got to his feet and moved forward to put his arm round Sandy. She pulled away and for a split second stood motionless. Then she lunged forward and slapped Nicole in the face.

The light blurred into a thousand pieces. Nicole put up a hand to her burning cheek and held it there until her vision cleared.

The couple at the next table leapt up. 'Is everything all right?' the man said.

'Very much all right,' said Sandy and stalked off, Bradley following.

Dazed, Nicole felt strong arms go round

193

her. Her heart did an involuntary little somersault as she realised who it was. 'Daniel?' she whispered, leaning against him for a comforting moment.

He held her close. 'I'm here, Nicole. Are you hurt?'

'No, no, really . . .'

'I'll beat the living daylights out of him.'

'No, Daniel, let it go.'

'Sure?' Releasing her, he looked at her anxiously. 'Are you certain you're all right?'

She nodded. His concern for her was heartening. 'It's the shock, that's all,' she said, trembling a little. She could hardly believe that she was emerging at last from a nightmare that had plagued her for weeks. It would take a while to sink in. 'Don't let Mark do anything, will you?'

'He'll just make sure they've cleared off, that's all.'

The waitress was back now, carrying a mug of steaming coffee, murmuring words of sympathy. 'On the house,' she said.

Daniel smiled. 'Sit down and drink it up, Nicole, there's a good girl.'

She did as he said and drank the coffee scalding hot. She felt a good deal better for it and for Daniel's caring company. By the time she had finished Mark was there, exchanging looks with Daniel and then smiling at Nicole and patting her hand.

'All finished now?' he said in approval for

a job well done. 'You won't be bothered by Bradley again.' He looked suddenly anxious. 'I put Daniel in the picture without telling you, Nicole. I hope you don't mind? I thought it better for you not to be too conscious of a bodyguard nearby in case that chap picked up on it.'

'Thanks for your support, both of you,' she said. She rubbed her cheek again, hoping Sandy had left no mark. But even if she had it would be worth it to be rid of Bradley for good. 'So where were you?'

'Lurking among the crowds,' said Daniel. 'I left my false moustache in my rucksack, though. I hope you don't mind.'

'You look nicer without it.'

Mark's eyes lit up as he smiled. 'I'll run you back to Kenvarloe when you're ready, Nicole. I need to see Zelda anyway.'

She hesitated. 'I'll stay on for a bit, but thanks,' she said. 'Will you explain everything to Zelda for me, Mark? She won't need to worry about me any more now.'

'I'll do better than that. I'll keep her company for the rest of the day and be ready to help out when needed, so take your time, Nicole. She'll be all right.'

She knew from his smile and the dreamy expression in his eyes that he would make sure that Zelda understood how things had changed for the better. Mark was a good man. He would make Zelda as happy as she deserved to be. They would have a lot to talk about and plan and she would keep out of their way today for as long as possible without making it obvious what she was doing.

She smiled. 'I'd like to take a look at *Flotsam Follies* and see the damage for myself,' she said.

She knew what to expect, but it was still a shock to see the place so derelict and unloved.

'A bit of a mess, isn't it?' said Daniel.

She stood in silence, moved beyond speech, gazing through the window at the blackened remains of Olaf's work. Daniel, too, looked thoroughly downcast. He had pinned so much on his ability to set Olaf and Pippa on the right path and now it had come to nothing.

'How can Olaf bear it?' she said at last. 'Pippa too.'

'Pippa hasn't seen it yet,' he reminded her.

'Olaf didn't want her to see it. He's protective of his sister.'

'It's always been the two of them against their father's strong will,' Daniel said. 'From what I gather Laurie Williams has been set against anything Olaf has wanted to do all his life.'

'That's really sad,' said Nicole. 'But now everything's changing if Olaf is offered the bird sanctuary job that his father set him up for.'

'Not his father,' Daniel said. 'Olaf.'

She turned to him in astonishment. 'Olaf

arranged this himself?'

'We had a long talk while Pippa was collecting wood that time I met them at Witten and Mark came ashore with his bucketful of mackerel. Olaf found out I had some connection with the wildlife centre at Pollack. There's a bird sanctuary nearby, you see. He's only just realised they need a warden and applied for the job straight away.'

'I see,' Nicole said doubtfully.

'Birds have always been his first love. His father, of course, put the boot in long ago. But now Olaf's going for it and Laurie Williams seems happy.'

Nicole smiled. 'So at long last Laurie Williams is respecting Olaf's wishes?'

'And Olaf appears to accept it with no recriminations. Good lad.'

Nicole was thoughtful. 'There's a lot I don't understand,' she said.

'Nor me,' said Daniel. 'Pippa seems to think her father's going to be at home more now. We can never understand other people entirely, can we? Poor *Flotsam Follies*!'

Nicole thought of her plans for Pippa to help out at the tearoom, perhaps even be more responsible for it in time, but said nothing. 'Sometimes we have to allow people to arrange things for themselves,' she said.

Daniel turned to look at her and in his eyes she saw something that made her heart leap.

They bought pasties at Daniel's favourite

shop together with cans of orange juice and two of the largest apples he could find. She laughed when she saw them, but Daniel ignored her amusement and insisted on adding them to the carrier bag of provisions he thought necessary for the picnic lunch he suggested they should share.

They took it all to the beautiful beach that Daniel had discovered when he set out along the coast path from Trevillick soon after they met. Here he had parked his rucksack and since it had been a hot day and his shorts were wet from his rescue mission, he had plunged into the waves that were a good deal bigger than they were today. The tide was in, too, and the expanse of soft sand much smaller.

He told Nicole something of this as they walked across to the far rocks to chose a spot to settle near some rock pools. 'It was exhilarating,' he said. 'And the sun was so hot I soon dried off completely so I didn't have to change into dry ones after all. I stayed for ages. That's why I took a long time to get to the Dancing Hole on the headland. Imagine my amazement to see you there when I hadn't expected to see you again.'

'I'm not surprised after the brush-off I gave you,' she said. 'It was Bradley, you see. You look a bit alike. I thought you were him.'

He frowned. 'I can't say I'm flattered.'

'But you're not like him now,' she assured him.

'Thank goodness for that,' he said in exaggerated relief as they settled themselves on the warm sand. 'Did he change or did I?'

Nicole removed her sandals and wriggled her toes, loving the feeling of freedom this gave her. 'I was the one who changed,' she said. 'I see far more clearly today. You're not a bit alike, Daniel, believe me. Bradley's selfish and vain and thinks only of himself.'

'And I don't?'

She smiled. 'Not so far.'

'You'll let me know if I let my standards slip?'

'If you're still around.'

'You won't get rid of me that easily.'

'Let's not think about Bradley any more. It's so perfect here. Look at that little brown bird perched on the rock over there. Oh it's off now, peep-peeping away.'

'A rock pipit,' said Daniel. 'It likes foraging among the rocks and seaweed. That's its alarm call.'

'Nothing to be alarmed about here.' She gave a sigh of pleasure. On the wet sand bordering the sea gentle ripples of water stirred and there wasn't a breath of wind. Only a couple of seagulls strutting about and eyeing them with interest disturbed their solitude. Later, she knew, this lovely beach would gradually fill up with people enjoying the sunshine, but by then they would be on their way.

'I'm hungry. I don't know about you?' Daniel passed her pasty to her in its paper bag.

Nicole took it from him and the steamy smell of meat, potato, swede and onion made her mouth water. 'If I wasn't before, I am now,' she said.

They ate in silence and when they had finished Daniel said, 'You haven't seen Mark's house, have you?'

She shook her head. 'Zelda says it's lovely and airy with huge windows looking over the sea. She'll be happy there, I know she will.'

'You're a kind girl, Nicole,' he said. 'Coming all the way down from London to help her out like you did.'

'And to avoid Bradley,' she reminded him.

'That too.'

He flipped open his can and took a long drink. She looked at him as he sat with his head thrown back and longed to kiss his tanned neck and smell the clean scent of him.

'And I admire you for giving up your time to help *Flotsam Follies*,' she said.

His eyes clouded. 'But it didn't do much good, did it? Failure's my middle name.'

She laughed. 'Dramatic idiot, more like,' she said.

'How come? Isn't it the truth?'

'You've helped Olaf see the way forward and Pippa to discover what she really wants to do. You've encouraged Zelda by finding the mackerel curry recipe for her. How's that for starters?'

'Well, yes . . .'

'And Laurie Williams seems to have come to his senses at last about his son. With luck Olaf will still make those lovely things in his spare time and he and Pippa will go beachcombing together. She'll like working for Zelda too.'

'Working for Zelda?'

Nicole told him what she envisaged for Pippa's immediate future.

'Hey,' he said when she had finished. 'I'm the one supposed to be giving a helping hand to the two of them.'

She laughed. 'Do you still regret what you did on that Crete holiday long ago?'

'No, my love. I don't regret it now.'

She let out a sigh of pleasure that she had heard him say it. 'I liked the way you talked about needing wild places every now and again to get everything into perspective. It made a lot of sense. You made me see how important it was to solve the Bradley problem once and for all and I want to thank you for that.'

'So I'm not a failure after all?'

'You know you're not, you idiot,' she said, her voice deep with emotion.

His eyes shone as he looked at her. For a glorious moment she felt the shimmering air around them shatter into a million pieces that came together again into a rush of love.

She clutched at the nearest rock and its

strength beneath her grip was satisfying. 'If it wasn't for Bradley we would never have met,' she said in wonder.

'How come?' he asked, his voice full of tenderness.

'It was the shock of his phone call that made me drop my mobile into the deep water and you were there to rescue it.'

'The right place and the right time.'

'And the right situation or you might have passed by.'

'Seeing you standing there, Nicole, I'd never have passed by. Anymore than I could bear to leave you and carry on with my walk once my shoulder healed.'

'So it was lucky that *Flotsam Follies* needed your help?'

He smiled. 'Wasn't it just?'

She laughed, understanding now how it had been for him. 'Oh, that reminds me,' she said. 'There's something I have to do.' She got up and felt in her pocket for the shell bracelet. Then she tossed it into the nearest rock pool.

Daniel sprang up too and together they watched it sink down below the strands of green seaweed.

'That's gone,' she said with satisfaction. 'And I never want to see it again.'

'I hope you'll want to see me again,' he said. 'Or who shall I take on honeymoon to Crete? I don't want to go alone.'

She laughed shakily. 'You won't have to.'

'So you'll come too, my darling Nicole?'

'Of course. Who else?'

As his warm lips descended on hers she knew this was what she had been waiting for since time began and she gave a long shuddering breath of sheer delight.